W9-BPK-492

Accla~~~~~~~~~~~.cobs

"Jacobs is a sublime storyteller."
—*Romantic Times BOOKclub*

And her recent titles

"You're in for a wild ride as you wonder if love
will prove to be the wisest ruler."
—*Romantic Times BOOKclub* on
Once Upon a Prince

"Holly Jacobs has masterfully penned
an absolutely delightful story..."
—*CataRomance.com* on *Once Upon a Princess*

"While *Be My Baby* showcases Holly Jacobs's
unique humor and wit, this story has more;
it has tender emotions that bring tears to
your eyes. It reveals the real meaning of
family and the healing power of true love."
—*Romance Reviews Today* on *Be My Baby*

Dear Reader,

July might be a month for kicking back and spending time with family at outdoor barbecues, beach cottages and family reunions. But it's an especially busy month for the romance industry as we prepare for our annual conference. This is a time in which the romance authors gather to hone their skills at workshops, share their experiences and recognize the year's best books. Of course, to me, this month's selection in Silhouette Romance represents some of the best elements of the genre.

Cara Colter concludes her poignant A FATHER'S WISH trilogy this month with *Priceless Gifts* (#1822). Accustomed to people loving her for her beauty and wealth, the young heiress is caught off guard when her dutiful bodyguard sees beyond her facade...and gives *her* a most precious gift. Judy Christenberry never disappoints, and *The Bride's Best Man* (#1823) will delight loyal readers as a pretend dating scheme goes deliciously awry. Susan Meier continues THE CUPID CAMPAIGN with *One Man and a Baby,* (#1824) in which adversaries unite to raise a motherless child. Finally, Holly Jacobs concludes the month with *Here with Me* (#1825). A heroine who thought she craved the quiet life finds her life invaded by her suddenly meddlesome parents and a man she's never forgotten and his adorable toddler.

Be sure to return next month when Susan Meier concludes her CUPID CAMPAIGN trilogy and reader-favorite Patricia Thayer returns to the line to launch the exciting new BRIDES OF BELLA LUCIA miniseries.

Happy reading!

Ann Leslie Tuttle
Associate Senior Editor

Please address questions and book requests to:
Silhouette Reader Service
U.S.: 3010 Walden Ave., P.O. Box 1325, Buffalo, NY 14269
Canadian: P.O. Box 609, Fort Erie, Ont. L2A 5X3

Here With Me

Holly Jacobs

SILHOUETTE *Romance*®

Published by Silhouette Books

America's Publisher of Contemporary Romance

To all the Perry Square readers who've supported these
stories, from *Do You Hear What I Hear?* on, thank you.
This one's for you.

And to the staff at the Harlequin Distribution Center.
I had so much fun visiting with you. Thanks for
all the wonderful work you do!

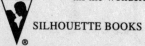 SILHOUETTE BOOKS

ISBN-13: 978-0-373-19825-2
ISBN-10:   0-373-19825-6

HERE WITH ME

Copyright © 2006 by Holly Fuhrmann

Visit Silhouette Books at www.eHarlequin.com

Printed in U.S.A.

HOLLY JACOBS

can't remember a time when she didn't read…and read a lot. Writing her own stories just seemed a natural outgrowth of that love. Reading, writing, chauffeuring kids to and from activities makes for a busy life. But it's one she wouldn't trade for any other.

Holly lives in Erie, Pennsylvania, with her husband, four children and a 180-pound Old English mastiff. In her "spare" time, Holly loves hearing from her fans. You can write to her at P.O. Box 11102, Erie, PA 16514-1102 or visit her Web site at www.HollyJacobs.com.

Dear Reader,

Here with Me is a special book for me in part because of Lee and Adam. Theirs is a story about balance. Balancing work and family. Balancing wants and needs. Balancing past and present. Balancing a dream with reality. Both need to find that balance, and they must discover where their true home is. Is it a house, a brick-and-mortar sort of place, or could it be that home truly is where the heart is?

My family moved from our house of thirteen years not long ago. Two of my children had never lived anywhere else. I'll admit, though I loved the new house, it didn't feel like home. Then one day, I looked at my family sitting around the dinner table and I had my epiphany... I was home because they were here.

The fact that my discovery parallels my characters', that I get to examine the world, my life, through another's eyes is why I've been a reader all my life, and why I became a writer. I hope Lee and Adam's story speaks to you, as well!

Holly

Prologue

Mary Eileen Singer crept from her grandmother's house before the sun rose on her tenth birthday, just as the first pink rays danced over the lake. Even though it was August, the morning air was cool. The ground felt wet beneath her bare feet, which was just perfect.

She bent, ran her hands over the damp grass, then raised them to her face and scrubbed.

"Ah, there's something magic in that first dew. Back in Ireland they said if you washed your face in it, the next man you'd meet you'd someday wed. There's something magic about becoming a woman, too. You put those two wee bits of magic together and you have something special," her grandmother had said the night before.

Her grandmother had been right about so many things that Mary Eileen fully expected to soon meet this man whom she'd one day marry.

"When you've washed your face in the morning dew, you'll see him and you'll know," Grandma had promised.

Face duly washed, Mary Eileen hurriedly ate her breakfast and dressed carefully. It wouldn't do to meet the man she was going to marry looking less than her best.

She went and sat out in front of the cottage on her favorite rock, waiting for him.

Waiting was no hardship. Her grandmother's small cottage overlooked the lake. Not the well-tamed sandy beaches that lined Lake Erie's penin-sula, Presque Isle, farther to the west, but a rocky, wild section of shoreline east of the city.

As she sat, she daydreamed about her soul mate. He'd be tall and he'd smile a lot. He'd want nothing more than to spend all his time with her. He wouldn't work long hours as her parents did and he'd…

Her imagined list of future-husband dos and don'ts were interrupted by a voice calling her name.

"Mary, Mary Eileen."

Panic swamped her as she recognized the voice. What had she done?

This couldn't be the magic.

Oh, yes she knew that voice. She was waiting for the man she was going to marry, not for Matty Benton. There was no way she was going to marry him someday.

She covered her eyes with her hands. Hoping that if she didn't actually see him, she'd be safe from the magic.

She heard his feet crunch the ground as he approached.

"Mary Eileen, what are you doing?"

She pressed her hands harder against her eyes so that not even the slightest sliver of light penetrated. "Nothing for you to worry about, Matty Benton."

"I came to see you," he said.

"Well, I can't see you today." She tried to think of an explanation for her covered eyes and finally said, "I had stuff put in my eyes at the doctor's and can't open them until tomorrow. If I look at the sun, I could go blind."

"Oh." He paused and said, "I'm sorry."

"Thank you. You can go now."

Even at ten, Mary Eileen knew she was being more than a little rude, but the longer Matty stayed, the greater the risk. No way did she want to marry him. Not horrible old Matty Benton. If she had to be mean in order to prevent it, she would be.

"That's what I came to tell you, I am going. I'm leaving Erie."

"Leaving?" she echoed.

Matty was a pain. He'd moved in with the Johnsons a year ago and was two years older than she was. He should spend his time willingly ignoring her like the rest of the older neighborhood kids did, but Matty wasn't the type to do what he *should* do. So not only did he not ignore her, he seemed to live to tease her.

She hated that, but it didn't mean Mary Eileen wanted him to leave.

"Yeah. Social Services found my dad's brother. My uncle Paul. He lives in New York City, so I'm moving there."

"Oh." New York City seemed worlds away from the sleepy beach outside Erie. "Are you glad?"

There was a small rush of air and Mary could almost picture Matty's characteristic shrug.

"Doesn't much matter," he said.

But it did matter.

She knew it did, even if Matty wouldn't say so.

"I'm sorry, Matty," she said softly.

It was her birthday and she was going to meet the man she'd marry. She should be celebrating, but instead, she felt sad and realized it was because she'd miss Matty Benton. He might be a pain, but there were occasions, like now, when he wasn't teasing her and she sort of liked him.

"What have I told you about calling me *Matty?*" he asked, his voice all deep and scary.

Matty had never scared her a bit. Annoyed, yes, but not scared. She laughed at his attempt to do so now. "*Matty's* better than *Matt*. There's just no way you're a Matt."

"Everyone else and their brother calls me *Matt*."

"They're wrong." She paused a minute and added, "But you're right. You're not exactly a Matty either."

"So who am I?" he asked.

"I don't know." And she felt a wave of loneliness that he was leaving and she'd never get to find out just what his name should be.

"Sorry about your eyes," he said.

She felt guilty for that lie. "Sorry you're leaving." She thought about telling him she'd miss him, but she couldn't quite get the words out.

There was another slight rustling of the air, and she knew Matty had moved. Something soft brushed against her cheek.

Matty Benton had kissed her.

Right after that thought, she heard the sound of rapid footsteps down the small stone path.

The gate creaked. "Bye, Mary Eileen. There's not much I'll miss about Erie, but I'll miss you. I left you something on the fence post."

"Bye, Matty."

And though she knew she shouldn't, though she

knew she was tempting fate, she cracked her inter-laced fingers the merest smidgen and peeked at the boy who was walking away.

"Goodbye, Matty."

Chapter One

"No, Mom, I'm fine. Nothing's wrong…. I like my life just the way it is." Lee Singer wished she could hang up. But hanging up wasn't an option, so she worked at tuning out her mother's you-could-do-so-much-better lecture. After all, she'd heard it so many times she could almost quote it verbatim.

So much potential, blah, blah, blah.

Wasting your life, blah, blah, blah.

If only you had some drive, some ambition, blah, blah, blah.

Mid-lecture, the door opened at Lee's small Perry Square art shop, Singer's Treasures, and a man walked in.

Her conversation with her mother faded to mere background static as she studied the customer with an uncharacteristic feminine awareness.

It wasn't that she didn't notice good-looking men, it was just that most of the time she didn't get hit with this sudden zing.

The man in question was tall. At five-six, she wasn't a tiny woman, but he towered over her. Six-two maybe?

Black hair, not a strand out of place, dark eyes that didn't look as if they missed anything. He was dressed in a neatly pressed polo shirt and Dockers. He wasn't exactly scowling, but he wasn't exactly smiling either.

No, he was sort of studying her with an intensity that made her very…

She searched for a word to describe the heart-pounding, blood-roaring feeling his scrutiny gave her. A word to describe how looking at him made her feel.

Desire.

That was it.

Not that she'd act on it. Lee believed herself to be the type of woman who knew that what was on the inside mattered more than how a person was packaged. But this man's packaging was a sight to behold.

She tried to steady her thoughts and her heart rate, and managed to say, "Pardon me a sec, Mom.

A customer just walked in." She put a hand over the phone's mouthpiece. "May I help you?"

"I came about a rental property on Lake Erie. I saw the ad in the paper and it said to contact Singer's Treasures."

She uncovered the phone and said, "Listen, Mom, I've got to go."

"I wasn't finished," her mother said. "Your father and I have a surprise. We're—"

Her mother would never be finished because they were never going to see eye to eye on Lee's life choices. She had realized that long ago, but she couldn't help but wish her relationship with her mother was different.

"Sorry, Mom, but business calls. And business is supposed to be my priority. Remember? Send my love to Dad."

Before her mother could utter any further protests, Lee clicked off the power on the portable phone, then set it on the counter.

"I'm sorry," she apologized. "Parents. You know how they are."

"Not really," the man said.

From his expression she could tell she'd made a faux pas.

"I'm sorry," she offered, though she wasn't sure what she was sorry for. She decided to take her mother's advice and for once be all business. "You wanted to know about the cottage I have to rent."

He nodded, still studying her.

"It's small, a one bedroom that sits on the lake. It has great views, if you like the water. I usually rent it out by the week. Plumbing, electricity…the basics, but not very fancy."

A man this pressed and preppy on a hot, humid summer day was the type who was used to fancy… demanded fancy, even.

Her small cottage probably wouldn't suit him at all.

"Is it vacant?"

She nodded.

"Good. I'll take it for a month." He reached in his pocket and pulled out a checkbook.

"But you haven't even seen it," Lee protested, knowing it wasn't a very businesslike response.

He ignored her. "How much for a month?"

Lee thought quickly. She'd never been overly aggressive about renting the cottage out and never for an entire month.

The cottages were built by her grandmother and her great-aunt on lakefront property years ago. They stood side-by-side overlooking Lake Erie. Lee now lived in her grandmother's cottage and rented out its twin.

She wasn't sure she wanted this man living next to her that long. The feelings he stirred were not conducive to a quiet, happy summer.

Tense. That's how she felt. Like a string on a bow, pulled taut.

A string that hadn't been pulled in far too long.

A string she wasn't sure she wanted pulled.

She named an absurd rate that amounted to what she'd made all of last year renting the cottage out sporadically.

He didn't blink an eye. Didn't even pause. He just started writing in his checkbook.

"What are you doing?" she asked.

"Paying in advance." He paused and looked up. "I assume you're not going to object to the month's rent up front, are you?"

"No, but I… I mean…"

"How do you want the check made out? To you personally, or to the store?"

"Either way," she said weakly, unsure how he'd managed to rent a cottage she wasn't sure she wanted to rent to him.

"If I'm going to make it out to you personally, what name should I use?"

"Lee," she said. "Uh, Lee Singer."

"Lee?" He sounded surprised.

"Yes. And I suppose if you're going to be renting the cottage, I should know your name."

"Adam," he said, then waited half a beat, watching her intently again. "Adam Benton."

He thrust out his hand, obviously ready to shake on the deal.

But the funny thing was, Lee absolutely didn't want to shake his hand…didn't want to touch him at all. Not because he was scary, but because he wasn't. Not the least bit.

After her disastrous marriage, she'd sworn off men. But for this one, she might reconsider. And that's why she didn't want to touch him.

Unfortunately, she couldn't think of any way out of it. So she took his hand, gave it one quick shake, then pulled back. That small bit of contact made her feel as if she'd been running a marathon. Her heart was racing, her palms were sweaty and her mouth was dry.

She nervously fingered her necklace.

"What's that?" he asked, peering at her neck.

She dropped her hand, hoping he'd shift his attention. "Nothing. It's just a nervous habit."

"No, the necklace. It looks unusual."

"Oh." She pulled the small glass rectangle out so he could see it. "It's one of my necklaces. It's what Singer's Treasures is known for."

She pointed down at the glass case filled with jewelry.

Her small Perry Square store specialized in jewelry made from small bits of glass, polished smooth by the lake. Blues, browns, greens and translucent.

Lee took the glass and fashioned it into all kinds of interesting pieces. Earrings, necklaces, bracelets.

In addition to the jewelry, the store sold other trinkets. Small driftwood carvings. Paintings of the lake. Most of the work was hers, although she did display other people's pieces on consignment.

But the lake was the theme that ran through all the treasures in the store.

Lake Erie was her inspiration.

Her home.

She realized the man, Adam, was studying her again. It was almost as if he was looking for something. She wasn't sure what.

She dropped her necklace and tried to get back to the business at hand. "Before I cash your check, you should take a look at the cottage to be sure it will suit."

"You made all these?" he asked, studying the contents of the case and ignoring her comment.

"Yes. Now, about the cottage. You're sure you don't want to see it first?"

He tilted his head, then smiled a slow upturn of his lips. Rather than making him look less intimidating, it made him look even more so.

"I'm sure," he said in a low, smooth voice. "You see, I'm the kind of man who knows what he wants, then goes after it. And right now I need someplace quiet to figure a few things out. Your cottage on the lake should be just right."

She wasn't sure how to respond to that, so she simply said, "Oh. Well, thank you."

"The key." There was the slightest hesitation, then he added her name, "Lee."

"Oh, right." She rummaged through her desk drawer and withdrew the key. "Here you go. And if you wait, I'll copy you directions. It's about twenty minutes from here."

"Don't bother. I know the way."

"But how?" she asked.

He ignored the question. "I'll be moving in to-morrow. Thank you."

He turned and headed out of the shop, stopped abruptly and turned. "I'll be seeing you, Lee."

Again, there was a weird pause as he said her name.

"Yes, you will, you see—" She started to tell him she lived next door, but he simply turned and left.

She looked at the check.

Adam Benton.

It listed a New York address.

Her grandmother used to say everything always happens for a reason. Lee couldn't help wondering just what reason Adam Benton had for renting her cottage.

And even more, she couldn't help but wonder about her out-of-character reaction to him. There was something about him…something more than just attraction. Almost a familiarity.

She shook her head. That was silly. She'd cer-tainly remember meeting a man like Adam Benton.

And yet the feeling nagged at her. There was something about him.

Well, she'd have the next four weeks to figure it out.

The thought wasn't very comforting.

Her new tenant had been gone less than ten minutes when the front door of the shop opened again.

"Now, that was a fine lookin' man if I ever saw one," Pearly Gates, Perry Square's version of a town crier, said as she strode into the shop. "He met up with some woman and baby in the park after he left here. The three of them got into an SUV and drove off."

"That's nice," Lee said, not knowing what else Pearly was after, but knowing there would be something.

"So who is he?" Pearly, a spry, grey-haired woman with a touch of the south in her voice, pulled a stool up to the glass case that held Lee's jewelry and waited for her explanation.

"Why would you think he was anything except a customer?" Lee asked, rather than answering.

"A customer doesn't spend nigh on twenty minutes pacin' up and down the block. He paused in front of your door at least half a dozen times and I'd think, there he goes, he's goin' in. But he wouldn't. He'd just walk down the block again. Looked to me like he was workin' up his nerve."

"I can't imagine why. Maybe he was just trying to get a feel for the neighborhood."

"Ha," Pearly said, not a bit convinced. "He didn't look like someone coming from the police station, and he barely slowed his gait when he walked by the

Five and Dine. Misty says today's a cinnamon-roll day. Who can resist slowin' up to smell that? No, he was working up his nerve for something. And I want to know what it was."

"How do you know what's going on over here? I'm across the park from Snips and Snaps for goodness sake. Do you have a telescope over there or something?"

"Good eyes. It's genetic. My great-grandmother Hazel lived to be ninety-eight and never needed glasses. She claimed she didn't need hearing aids either, but the woman was deaf as a post. Did I ever tell you about the time she—"

The shop's door opened again and a couple came in, interrupting Pearly's story. Which was sort of a relief as Pearly's stories could easily take an entire afternoon for the telling, what with all the twists, turns and tangents she put in them.

"Welcome to Singer's Treasures," Lee called out. "Let me know if I can assist you in any way."

"Thank you," the woman said.

"Well, Pearly, I guess that story's going to have to wait."

"Fine. You can dodge the story of how Hazel lost her bloomers on Main Street, but only if you tell me about the mystery man."

Lee should have just admitted defeat the first time Pearly had asked. To the best of her knowledge, no one had ever dodged her for long.

"His name's Adam Benton. He rented my cottage." Again, a feeling of familiarity swept over her as she mentioned his name.

She had to be imagining a connection. After all, what woman in her right mind wouldn't want a connection to a gorgeous man like Adam Benton?

"He's staying out at your place?" Pearly asked.

Lee could just imagine how Pearly could distort that particular slant on the story, so she quickly tried to set it to right. "Not my place, the other cottage."

"Well, well, well." Pearly studied her a moment, then broke out in a huge grin. "Well, I do like the sound of that. Another Perry Square match could be in the making."

"You said he had a woman and a baby in the park. He's probably married and bringing the whole family out."

"Nah. He didn't touch the lady once. He just nodded at her when he came out of here. I don't think there's anything between them."

"They probably were just fighting, or maybe she had all she could do to handle the baby."

"Or maybe it was his sister and niece, and he's single. I like the sound of a nice-looking, single man living with you."

"Not *with* me, next to me." Pearly looked as if she were going to argue, so Lee continued, "Don't get any ideas, Pearly Gates. Just because you're in love, doesn't mean I will be. I've tried a relationship in the past, and it's obvious I don't have what it takes. Plus, I like my life just as it is."

Pearly had come back from a trip to Europe with a new boyfriend. Not quite a new boyfriend. An old boyfriend she'd rediscovered. Their story was the talk of the Square.

Pearly had gone to a small European country, Eliason, for a wedding, and had discovered her childhood sweetheart had been an ambassador to the country for years before he'd retired. They'd picked up their tumultuous relationship and when Pearly had come back to Perry Square, the ambassador had followed.

"Sure, you love your life," Pearly said, still grinning. "I loved mine as well. But even though finding my Buster has changed it, it's a change for the better."

"Pearly—" Lee started to warn her, but at that moment her customers came up and asked about a painting. While she answered them, Pearly sneaked out.

The coward.

Lee didn't even want to hear the rumors that would be flying up and down the square before tomorrow's breakfast.

Pearly Gates would make a mountain out of this molehill.

Another match?

Ha.

Perry Square might have had a number of matches of late, but Lee Singer wasn't about to join the ranks. She was wise enough to learn from her mistakes.

There was absolutely no way she was matching with anyone.

Not even if her new tenant was one of the best-looking men she'd seen in a long time.

The next day, Adam Benton got out of his SUV and breathed deeply, then exhaled slowly. He studied the twin cottages. They looked exactly as he remembered them. Two one-story buildings with well-weathered clapboard siding and huge front porches complete with rockers and tables.

As he drank in the sight, he felt as if he were coming home, which was ridiculous. Home was New York.

This?

The cottage just outside Erie in Northeast Pennsylvania was just a place where he used to live near this girl he used to know.

And that girl, Mary Eileen Singer, had never really liked him much.

He smiled and acknowledged she had every right not to like him. He'd tormented her with all the gusto a young boy could.

A loud squawk from the back of the SUV announced that Jessie was ready to be set free.

"Hey, there, kiddo," he said as he worked the myriad of hooks and buckles that locked the baby into the car seat.

Actually, now that Jessie was mobile, he should probably start thinking of her as a toddler.

"Here we go," he said as he lifted her out of the car.

Jessie immediately arched her back, her nonverbal cue that she didn't want to be held. He set her down and she squealed with delight.

"Don't eat the grass," he warned as her chubby fingers grabbed a large hunk and started pulling.

She giggled, not the least bit intimidated. "What on earth am I going to do with you?"

That's what this break was all about—figuring out what to do about Jessie.

He remembered all those years ago. His parents had died, and he'd gone to live with a foster family. Then one day, his social worker had announced she'd found his uncle, and that this unknown relative had agreed to let Adam come live with him.

He hadn't been thrilled about going to New York. But over time, he and Paul had sort of meshed. Adam had continued living with his uncle while he'd gone to college and things had been great. Two single guys in the city.

A year after Adam started, Paul met Cathie.

Adam remembered those first few months Paul had dated her. Adam had been obnoxious.

That seemed to be a theme in his past—obnoxious.

He hoped he'd grown out of it.

He watched as Paul and Cathie's daughter picked the grass and let it run through her fingers.

She didn't seem to be too affected from her loss. Adam, on the other hand, was reeling from losing Paul and Cathie two months ago.

They were the only family he had—except for Jessie, their daughter. His cousin and goddaughter.

Adam Benton might know how to handle himself in the business world, but he wasn't equipped for this, for dealing with an eighteen-month-old.

Jessica Aubrey Benton was his responsibility.

Paul and Cathie had trusted him to raise her.

When the lawyer had told him, it had shocked him. He'd assumed they'd named Cathie's folks Jessie's guardians.

Cathie's parents had assumed the same and had been equally shocked.

But Paul and Cathie had named him guardian in their will. Their choice still didn't make sense to Adam. But he'd picked the toddler up from her grandparents just two weeks ago, determined to take some time with her and decide what to do.

He shook his head as he watched Jessie gleefully wiggle her fingers in the long grass.

Give him a room full of corporate execs. Give him a computer system that needed to be created from scratch…that he could deal with.

Even give him the new computer chip that he

hoped would put Delmark, Inc. on the road to success and he was in his element.

Yes, Adam Benton could cope and plan on par with just about anyone when it came to business matters.

But Jessie?

He just wasn't sure what to do with her.

He loved her, but he wasn't prepared for taking over her care on his own.

After the will had been read, Cathie's parents had immediately started pressuring him to let them have her and raise her. Part of him agreed it was the best idea. The other part felt obligated to honor Paul's request.

He was torn and needed time to sort out what was going to be best for Jessie.

But he wasn't going to figure anything out standing in the driveway. He got busy unpacking the car. Once he got Jessie's box of toys, she was content to play with them on the porch. As soon as she'd dumped the box, she'd drop them all back in, then start again.

He hadn't brought much. A few suitcases for each of them, his laptop, printer and fax machine, and Jessie's toys and her portable crib.

When everything was in the living room, he scooped up Jess and her toys, and she played while he set up the crib in the bedroom. As soon as it was up, he laid her down. She must have been tired because she was almost agreeable as she settled down for her nap with just a token of a complaint.

Adam cracked her bedroom window so he could

hear her, and went out to the front porch. It had two rockers on it, just as it always had. They looked weathered enough to be the same two that had sat here years before.

Nothing about the twin cottages on the lake seemed to have changed, unlike Mary Eileen.

Lee.

She'd changed her name.

Well, not really changed it, but altered it.

Not that he could find fault with that. He'd altered his as well.

He'd almost forgotten Mary Eileen Singer until he'd read an article a month ago. It talked about how a small shop on Perry Square was making big waves with its unique jewelry. He hadn't connected the girl he knew with the jewelry artist Lee Singer until he'd seen her picture. At the time, it had spurred a passing memory of his time in Erie.

But after he lost Paul and Cathie in the accident, he'd known Erie was the perfect place to get away and figure things out. He'd known that Lee would—

He broke off his thoughts of the past as a Jeep came down the long dirt driveway.

She was here.

Her shoulder-length brown hair was pulled into a casual ponytail. He knew if he were closer he could see the hints of red that threaded through its strands.

What he could never be sure of was how her eyes would look. They were the type of neutral color that seemed to change day to day, much like the lake. Sometimes almost blue, sometimes a dark gray that almost bordered on black.

She spotted him on the porch and waved. She didn't look overly excited to see him.

Well, that was one thing that hadn't changed, because Mary Eileen had never been overly enthused with his company, although she'd always been kind and polite.

It was that kindness he remembered the most.

Maybe that's why he'd returned? The article appearing the day before Paul and Cathie's accident—the day his world had tilted on its axis and changed so fast—seemed like a sign.

Maybe that's why he'd been drawn back to this spot. He needed something stable, something he could count on. This place was the only stable thing he could recall now that Paul and Cathie were gone.

Mary Eileen Singer's kindness was like that...dependable. He hadn't seen her in eighteen years, but he knew in his gut that quality about her hadn't changed.

"Mr. Benton," Mary Eileen called as she approached. "Are you all settled in?"

"Yes, thank you. I didn't bring much, so it didn't take long. It was nice of you to stop by and check on me," he said.

"I wasn't being nice. I started to tell you, before you so abruptly left—"

She was scolding him, he realized, and resisted

the urge to grin at the thought. He hadn't been scolded…well, in a very long time.

"—that I live in the cottage next to yours."

"I thought you might."

"But you left so fast that I didn't have a chance," she continued; then what he'd said hit her and she paused a moment, then asked, "What do you mean, you thought I might live here?"

He knew he should have told her earlier who he was when he first saw her again, but some devil of an inclination wanted to see if she'd recognize him.

She hadn't.

He should have felt a sense of satisfaction that he'd changed that much. He had worked hard to become Adam Benton, trying to leave the troubled boy he'd been behind.

He'd obviously succeeded.

And yet, he'd thought maybe Mary Eileen would see through his facade.

"I know, Mary Eileen, because I've been here before. Not for a long time, but I remember how much this place meant to you."

"What do you mean you've been here before? I would have…" She stopped a moment and stared at him.

"Matty Benton," she whispered.

She did remember.

He felt suddenly lighter than he had in a long time.

"You said I wasn't a Matt, and not really a Matty. What do you think of an Adam?"

She continued to study him and Adam felt a bit naked. Not in a no-clothes sense, but rather in a she-could-see-all-the-things-he'd-rather-keep-hidden sort of way.

She'd always made him feel like that.

But this was slightly different. Her study left him feeling more than a sense of coming home. It left him wanting to reach out and pull her into his arms.

He wondered how she'd react.

He doubted she'd melt into him and cover him with kisses.

No, he rather thought she'd deck him.

The thought made his smile broaden.

"Well?" he prompted.

She nodded slowly. "Yes, *Adam* suits you. It's who you are. Matthew Adam Benton."

"Adam Mathias Benton."

"Oh, la-di-da," she said with a laugh. "To be honest, that suits you even better."

"And you, Lee instead of Mary Eileen."

"*Mary Eileen* was a bit too long to fit on my artwork, so I started signing *Lee* and by the time I got to college it just stuck."

"It suits you as well."

"So, Adam," she smiled as she said his name, "what brings you back to Erie from New York?"

How to answer that.

There were a dozen different ways, and all of them would be accurate up to a point.

"Da!" Jessie cried in a voice so loud it was hard to believe it came from such a tiny body.

"Pardon me," he said, running into the cottage before Jessie tried to get out of the crib herself.

"Da," she repeated as he came into her room.

Da.

Short for *Adam*.

He was swept away by the memory of Cathie working with Jessie, trying to get her to say *Adam*. *Da* was as close as she'd come.

He tried not to think of his uncle's wife. Cathie had had a sense of happiness that had simply radiated in everything she'd done.

As he lifted Jessie out of the crib and she smiled at him, he was hit with a wave of regret that Paul and Cathie had missed that smile, just as they'd miss so many things in the coming years.

"Da," Jessie said and started a string of babble that he couldn't understand, but seemed of the utmost importance to Jessie.

"Come on, short stuff. I want to introduce you to someone." He took the baby to the porch, but Lee was gone.

"Maybe later then," he murmured to the baby.

Chapter Two

A baby was crying. But Lee was lost in her art. She was working on a new piece. Though she knew she should attend to the baby, she continued working. Ignoring everything but work…

Lee awoke from the nightmare drenched in sweat. She'd had variations of the dream before, but not in months. She didn't have to be a psychiatrist to figure out hearing Adam's baby today had triggered tonight's foray into the past.

Knowing she wouldn't be going back to sleep until she wound down, she got out of bed and stood at her bedroom window. It faced the other cottage.

Normally, the memories here in her grandmother's cottage helped keep the nightmares away. She looked at her cottage's twin. When she was very small, her great-aunt had lived there. Now, behind its door was Adam Benton.

Matty.

He must be why she'd been working on that particular piece of jewelry in her dream.

She turned away from the window and opened a small chest at the foot of her bed. It was stuffed with childhood mementos.

She pushed aside a high-school pennant, an old diary, and some photographs before she finally found what she was looking for. The small seashell-covered Popsicle-stick box she used to keep trinkets in was exactly as she remembered it. Inside was the first piece of beach-glass jewelry she'd ever made. The worn chip of clear glass was shaped like a heart. The piece she'd been working on in tonight's dream.

As she fingered it, she couldn't help remembering that last meeting with him so many years ago.

She got up and went back to the window. Eighteen years ago. She smiled remembering her grandmother's story about the dew. But no prince had ridden to find her that day, just Matty Benton announcing he was leaving for New York.

He'd left this small piece of glass on the fence post that day.

And now he was back.

Everything always happens for a reason.

Her grandmother had believed in things like destiny and magic. Even if she'd never set foot on the Irish shores, she'd been at heart an Irish woman with a gift for the blarney.

Magic does exist, she'd told Lee.

While her parents had been busy with work, busy chasing after their next big deal, her grandmother had told her stories of Ireland. She'd always had time for Lee.

Her mother and father had built big careers, while her grandmother had built love. Her parents were in Philadelphia now, still working day-in and day-out.

To Lee, *career* should be a four-letter word.

To this day, her parents frowned on Singer's Treasures.

After all, it wasn't a real job. She kept very short hours at the shop—noon to five—preferring to do most of her work here at the cottage. And recently, she'd hired someone to help out part-time.

Not a real job, was her parents' refrain. Her mother's lecture the other day had been much the same as all the others. There was no future in her work.

Try as she might, Lee had never been able to make them understand she worked to support her living; she didn't live to work.

There was a difference.

It was a difference they had never been able to appreciate.

A movement caught her eye. A curtain billowed at Adam's cottage.

Maybe the baby was up, scared to wake in the dark in a strange house. Maybe it had cried, prompting her dream.

Lee slid her window open, so she'd be able to hear any noise, but all she could hear was the familiar sound of waves lapping the shore.

She slipped a throw over her shoulders, made her way through the dark house that hadn't really changed since her childhood, and out onto the porch.

Still nothing.

It must have been her imagination.

She sank into one of the rocking chairs. Creaking it back and forth as she gazed out over the star-studded sky and the last traces of her nightmare faded, she lost herself in the natural beauty of the lake, remembering why she loved it here.

"Can't sleep?" came Adam's voice from the step.

She jumped. She hadn't heard him coming over. "You startled me."

"Sorry," he said, though he didn't sound overly contrite. He took the other rocker without waiting for an invitation.

They rocked together in companionable silence for quite a while.

Finally Lee said, "Won't your wife miss you?"

"I don't have a wife, Lee."

She wanted to ask who the woman in the park was

then, but she didn't. She simply asked, "Is your baby all right by herself?"

"The cottages sit so close to one another that I'm sure I can hear her if she calls. I left the window open. She'll holler if she wakes up again. You might have noticed, but she's not exactly quiet and subtle."

Lee laughed. "She does have a good set of lungs, as my grandmother used to say."

So where was the baby's mother? Lee burned with curiosity, but couldn't think of a way to ask without seeming as if she were prying. Pearly wouldn't hesitate just to ask, but Lee couldn't, so she said nothing.

The silence didn't feel awkward. They simply rocked and stared out at the dark expanse.

Adam was the first one to speak again. "I was sorry to hear when your grandmother passed away. She was a true lady."

It had been five years, but Lee still missed her grandmother's gentle presence in her life. "Thank you. How did you hear?"

"I have the Erie paper mailed to me in New York. I didn't want to lose my connection to this place. I had some happy memories here."

"Oh."

"I saw the article about Singer's Treasures last month. I didn't know you were the up-and-coming artist they were talking about until I saw your picture. You won the Jones Award for Art. That was impressive. I almost called to congratulate you."

"Really?" He'd followed her through the paper? She wasn't sure how she felt about that.

As if he sensed her feelings, he said, "It's not as if I got the paper to monitor you."

"I never thought that," she denied.

"You wondered if maybe I was some sort of stalker."

"No, I didn't."

He tsk-tsked.

Really, tsk-tsked, like Pearly Gates would tsk-tsk someone.

"You sound like an old woman," she said, teasing him. "Tsk-tsk, deary, and all that."

"Picking on me already, Singer? As I recall, you were always picking on me."

"Funny," she said, "I seem to remember it the other way around."

"Rather than argue who was the *pickee* and who was the *picker*, I'll say good night. Jessie gets up very early. She hates to miss out on anything by sleeping."

"Good night," Lee said.

She watched him walk back to his place. When his cottage door shut, she went back in as well and went to bed. When she finally slept, she dreamed the same dream she'd had regularly since that morning when she was ten.

A dark, shadowy figure of a man leaning down

toward her whispering her grandmother's words, "Magic does exist."

For the first time in a long time, she wished she could believe it were true.

The room was bright when Lee opened her eyes the next morning.

Way too bright.

And loud.

Normally the only sounds in the morning were the waves and maybe an occasional bird. Today, something was disturbing the usual peace and quiet.

Thump.

Thump.

Thump.

Lee groaned as she crawled out of bed. She'd tossed and turned all night—not because she'd had a repeat nightmare. Instead, every time she did manage to fall asleep, she saw him.

The dark man of her dreams.

It was disturbing.

Thump.

Thump.

Thump.

Her sleep-muddled mind slowly cleared and she realized that the noise was someone pounding at the door.

Pulling on an old robe, she went and opened it. Adam stood, holding his squirmy baby.

"I woke you," he said. "I'm sorry. Go back to bed." He turned around, as if he were going to leave.

"Don't be silly. It's way past time I was up. Do you want some coffee?"

"I'd love some, but I don't have time. I have a teleconference."

"It's Sunday."

"I know, but this last month has been crazy. The talk is about two weeks overdue, so I took it when I could. Unfortunately, I foolishly thought I could manage it with Jessie, but she's bent on exploring the new house. She's already unrolled all the toilet paper, emptied out the bottom cupboard, and—"

"I get the picture. You want me to watch her while you finish your meeting?"

"I was hoping you might. I mean, I know it's an imposition. I'd be happy to pay you. It's just this is important and I have to—"

Part of Lee wanted to say, *No…I don't do babies.* But Adam looked slightly desperate, and the toddler was adorable. Blond hair in a wild, Eienstein-ish style, with light blue eyes and a huge smile.

Just because Lee had decided not to have children didn't mean she couldn't enjoy other people's.

"Go ahead and go," she said. "I'm sure I can handle…" She paused. "Jessie, wasn't it?"

"Yes. Jessie." He handed her the baby.

Lee felt the old familiar stab of pain as she took Jessie in her arms. After all this time, she'd hoped the ache would lessen, but it hadn't. And she was beginning to suspect it never would.

Adam set a bag on the floor. "There are diapers, some Cheerios, some toys…"

"We'll figure it out. Just go."

"Thanks," he called as he sprinted back across the short bit of yard that separated the two cottages.

"Well," Lee said, studying the beautiful little girl in her arms. "Maybe I should introduce myself, Miss Jessie. I'm Lee. I knew your daddy way back when. He was Matty then. And though he might think you're a handful, let me assure you, he was worse."

The toddler babbled. Lee thought she caught an occasional real word in the mix, but she thought that might be wishful interpretation on her part.

"Want to help me make some coffee?" The next burst of babble seemed to be positive, so Lee assumed Jessie's answer was a yes.

"Good. I'm absolutely worthless without a jolt of caffeine in the morning."

Half an hour later, Lee had managed to dress… just barely. In the time it took her to slip a T-shirt over her head, Jessie had run across the hall to the bathroom and unrolled half the toilet-paper roll.

"My grandmother would have said, 'she's full of piss and vinegar, that one.' I never quite figured out what that meant, but having met you, I believe I have an inkling."

Jessie didn't seem to take offense. She started shredding the long string of paper into smaller gobs.

"I think it might be better if we found something to entertain you," Lee said. "Let's go for a walk on the beach."

Jessie cooed her agreement and Lee scooped her up. She was enveloped in the scent of freshly washed baby again. She inhaled deeply and felt tears well in her eyes as an all too familiar pain asserted itself.

She brushed the tears away and tried to ignore all the what-could-have-beens as she concentrated on the what-was.

And *what-was* today was a beautiful blue sky, a warm spring sun and Jessie, who seemed eager to embrace her new temporary home.

"Come on, Jessie," Lee said, and they left the cottage.

Adam was pacing. He knew that it wouldn't help, but he had so much nervous energy.

Where could Lee have taken Jessie?

He shouldn't have trusted Jessie with her. He'd known Lee years ago, but he had no way of knowing what kind of woman she'd grown into.

What a fool.

Maybe he should call the police. It had been over an hour since he'd gone into his bedroom, shut the door and taken his conference call. Almost two hours since he'd left Jessie with Lee. Who knew—

Just then he spotted her climbing up the small hill, Jessie in her arms.

"Where were you?" Adam barked, his tone sharp, his expression angry as he rushed toward them.

"We went for a walk. What's wrong?" Lee asked, looking confused.

"What's wrong? I left Jessie with you and come back to find you've both disappeared. I spent the last hour worried sick."

"Oh, Adam, I'm sorry. I didn't mean to be that long. It's just—it was such a beautiful day and the beach sort of called me. Walking out wasn't a problem. But coming back was. I didn't realize how heavy Jessie could be. She might toddle about, but she's not exactly up to walking on her own. So we took breaks. Frequent breaks."

Jessie called, "Da," and held her arms out to him.

As he took her from Lee, his heart rate slowly returned to normal and he felt as if he could breathe again. He met Lee's eyes. "I'm sorry, too. I guess I overreacted. It's just that if anything were to happen to her…"

He let the sentence trail off. Nothing would ever happen to Jessie. He'd see to it. "I guess we should be going. I have work to do."

"Okay," Lee said, her tone subdued. "Really, I'm sorry to have given you a scare. My parents would tell you that I'm totally hopeless about time, and I'm as irresponsible as they come."

Adam didn't comment on her parents' opinion, even though he felt a flash of sympathy. He'd only seen them occasionally when he'd lived in Erie. It was Lee's grandmother who'd attended school functions—her grandmother he remembered.

He didn't say any of that. "No, I'm the one who's sorry. I lost my head. Thank you for watching her. I hope we didn't hold you up."

"Not at all. It was my pleasure." Her voice sounded stiff, and she didn't wait for him to respond. She just turned and walked into her cottage, shutting the door quite firmly behind her.

"Great," he muttered to the baby. "Looks like I've offended the only person I know in town."

Even as he said the words, he knew that wasn't why he felt like such a schmuck.

After all these years he'd hoped he and Lee had moved beyond the tease-and-torture stage, but maybe not.

"Come on, sweetie. Let's go home."

Chapter Three

Later that afternoon, Lee was distracting Adam. Not by anything she was actively doing, because she wasn't actually doing anything. She'd simply been sitting on the rock at the edge of the water for the longest time. She was staring at the lake, apparently lost in thought.

Adam was supposed to be lost as well. Lost in work that was piled in front of him on his makeshift desk, known as the kitchen table. A kitchen table near a window that overlooked the lake. For some reason, the files on his laptop didn't seem nearly as interesting as the woman in his sights.

Little Mary Eileen had grown into a beautiful woman.

He wondered if she was dating anyone, then realized it didn't matter. He might be interested, but even though she was available, and was easily the most intriguing woman he'd met—well, not met, but remet—in years, he didn't have time for a woman in his life.

He had Jessie.

He had decisions to make.

He had a business to worry about. Though Delmark, Inc. was in capable hands with Darius, his vice-president, at the helm, relinquishing control was foreign to Adam, so he was still trying to keep his eye on things, even long distance.

The company primarily worked on developing new computer systems. But recently, they'd developed an idea for a new processor. After they'd filed for a patent, they'd been inundated with offers for it. They could sell the rights, and make a tidy profit, or they could start an offshoot of Delmark and produce the chips themselves.

Adam was leaning toward expanding the company and producing and marketing the chips themselves. Delmark was on the cusp of a huge change.

It really wasn't the ideal time to be away from the company, but Jessie had to be his priority. The chip wasn't going anywhere. There was time for those decisions. But she deserved to have her future settled as soon as possible. Should he keep her, or let her live with her grandparents?

They were in their early seventies, but still active. Could they keep up with Jessie?

If he decided to retain custody, could he balance Jessie's needs with Delmark's?

By the time he left Erie next month, he'd have an answer.

Jessie bellowed that her naptime had ended. It was almost a relief to shut down the laptop. He went to retrieve her from her crib.

"Hey, there, mighty lungs," he murmured as he got her up. "How about a diaper change, then we can head outside?"

She gurgled her agreement to his plan. "Da," she added.

"Adam," he repeated, which made her smile.

He redressed her as she continued crooning, "Da, da, da."

"We need to work on your vocabulary, little girl," he said as they walked out of the cottage. Without giving it any thought, he automatically headed toward Lee, who was still sitting on the rock.

"Hello," he called.

It took her a moment to respond, but she turned and smiled. "Hello, yourself."

"I wondered if you'd let me buy you lunch as a thank you for watching Jessie this morning, and as an apology for my behavior before."

He hadn't planned to ask—had just decided he didn't have time for a woman, in fact—but as the words slipped out, he realized there was nothing more that he wanted to do than spend an afternoon with Lee.

"That's not necessary. No harm, no foul."

"Still, I'd like to."

"I was going to head into the Square. I finished a piece for a client and want to get it to the shop so she can pick it up."

"Do you have to work?"

"I recently hired someone and with her there, I've been working in the showroom less and less. I make most of the pieces here at home."

"And you have nothing pressing that you have to do today?"

"Just deliver that one piece," she admitted slowly.

"Well, I could ride in with you and once you drop it off, we could get something to eat in town when you're done."

She shook her head, causing the sun to bounce off her highlights. "Really, it's not necessary."

"You do eat, right?" he teased.

He wasn't sure why he didn't just accept her no and leave her in peace. All he knew was he really wanted to spend time with Lee, to get to know the woman the girl he'd known had grown into.

She smiled. "Yes, I eat on occasion."

"Well, oddly enough, so do I. You can show me around town. I haven't been back since I left for New York all those years ago."

"And now you've brought your daughter back."

"Cousin," he corrected.

Lee paused a moment, then repeated, "Cousin?"

"The uncle I left to live with?" Adam felt a stab of pain, a hollowness as he thought about Paul and Cathie. He pushed it aside. "Jessie's his daughter."

"Oh."

He thought she might ask why he had the baby, but she didn't. She got up, took a few steps, then turned around and said, "So, are you coming?"

He pushed the pain back into the recesses and grinned. "Absolutely."

His cousin. The baby was his cousin. He'd already admitted that he wasn't married.

Lee had wanted to ask why the baby was with Adam, but she'd seen he was hurting as he'd talked about his uncle and she didn't want to intrude on whatever his sorrow was.

She reached in her pocket and touched that small heart-shaped piece of glass. She'd meant to tuck it back in her memento box, but instead had put it in her pocket. She wasn't sure why. Until Adam had shown up, she'd practically forgotten the small bit of glass that had nudged her in a direction that was now her livelihood.

As they drove into Erie, Lee kept up a rolling commentary on changes and sites in the area, not because she thought he was interested, but because she felt the need to fill the silence.

"I'll drop this off at the store. It'll only take me a moment, then we can go to lunch," she stated, having exhausted her travelogue.

"No problem. Jessie and I have no plans for the rest of the day."

He got the baby out of her car seat, went to the back of the SUV and, one-handed, pulled out a stroller.

"Do you need help?" Lee asked.

"Jessie and I are getting this down to a science. The first few weeks she was with me, I was a mess, but I've learned to do a lot of things."

"So she hasn't been with you long then?"

He put Jessie in the stroller and busied himself buckling her in.

"My uncle and his wife were in an accident two months ago. I figured Cathie's parents would take Jessie, but Cathie and Paul named me Jessie's guardian. That's why I'm here. I've taken the month off from work so I can try to figure out what to do. Jessie's grandparents have asked to have her and part of me knows they'd probably do a better job, but then I bump into the fact Paul asked me to do it. He trusted me. I don't know if I can turn my back on that, on the other hand I don't know if I can balance work and playing single cousin. She's the only relative I have left in the world."

Lee reached out and touched his forearm. "I'm sorry."

He nodded, accepting her concern as empathy rather than pity.

"And since you don't have to make any decisions today, let's just concentrate on having some fun. If you have time, we could maybe take Jessie to the zoo after lunch. I've read about all their new additions, but haven't visited."

He smiled despite the ache in his heart. "We have time."

"Great. Then come on, we've got a full day ahead of us."

"I know I was in the store the day I rented the cottage, but I'd like a full tour."

"Sure." She held the door for Adam, who was pushing the stroller.

"Hi, Juliet," she called out to the young brunette behind the counter. "I brought Mrs. Ramsey's piece."

"Great. She called…again." Juliet Myers eyed Adam and Jessie. "Are you going to introduce me?"

"Juliet, this is Adam and Jessie."

"Nice to meet you," she said to Adam, then in a soft voice for Lee's ears only she added, "Way. To. Go."

Lee glanced over her shoulder, but Adam didn't appear to have overheard. He was spinning a beach-glass wind chime for Jessie.

"It's not like that," Lee snapped.

"Uh-huh. Tell me another one. Pearly's already

alerted the whole Square." Louder she said, "I'm going in the back to call Mrs. Ramsey. She'll be thrilled."

"She seems nice," Adam said, coming up behind Lee as she stood, sputtering silently, wanting to set things straight with both Juliet and Pearly.

Okay, maybe there would be no setting things straight with Pearly. Once the older woman made up her mind, there was no unmaking it. But surely Juliet could do a bit of damage control on Lee's behalf.

"Juliet is nice. Unfortunately, she doesn't really have a handle on the whole boss-employee relationship thing."

"I've got employees like that as well."

As Adam chuckled, Lee felt a sense of camaraderie. "Even if she doesn't realize I'm the boss. I originally hired her for just one afternoon a week, and now she's in the store more than I am sometimes. I don't know what I did without her."

"I'm sure you did just fine," Adam assured her. "The store is wonderful. So tell me about it."

"Well, let's see, I make most of the pieces, although we do sell some on commission for other local artists."

He turned and tapped the wind chime again, making Jessie squeal with glee. "Where do you get your glass? You can't collect all this on the beach yourself."

"I do collect some, but we also purchase it from

people who bring it in. It's a popular summer hobby for a number of locals. Especially young kids looking to earn a bit of pocket change."

"And then you turn the bits of glass into art like this," he said nodding at several wind chimes hanging nearby.

"That's a new idea. Mainly I make jewelry, but I was at a friend's and she had these loud wind chimes, and I thought if only they were softer, then I…" She shrugged, sure that Adam wouldn't be interested in the intricacies of the process.

"Then you had a strike of inspiration and made this?"

She nodded.

"I think Jessie's hooked. We'll take it."

Adam's cell phone rang as Lee packed the chimes. The sound brought back memories of her ex; he'd worked in real estate. His cell phone was never turned off because he was afraid he'd miss a commission. It often felt as if it never stopped ringing.

Lee tamped down her feelings of irritation. Adam wasn't her ex; he was just an old friend in town for a month. How he mixed business and his personal life was up to him.

Juliet walked back into the room. "Mrs. Ramsey is on her way over. You'd best make your escape while you can."

Lauralee Ramsey was a valued customer and a very sweet woman, but she was a talker. The woman could hold her own against Pearly Gates, and that was saying something.

"Thanks for the warning. Can you finish packing the chimes? Adam wants it. We'll pick it up after lunch."

"Blarney Scone or Monarch's?" Juliet asked.

Adam snapped his cell phone shut and said, "Did someone mention food?"

"Do you have a preference?" Lee asked.

"As long as I don't have to cook it, I'm pretty easy going."

"Then I think it's Monarch's. We can grab a quick sandwich before we take Jessie to the zoo."

"Great," Juliet bubbled. "Parker's back from the big wedding and honeymoon. The place is bustling with groupies wanting a chance to congratulate her in person."

"Groupies?" Adam asked.

"Turns out, Parker's a princess," Juliet told him as she continued wrapping the chimes. "She and her two friends opened Titles, the bookstore, and Monarch's coffeehouse. But now Cara and Shey are in Europe being all princessy. So Parker, who doesn't really care for the whole princess thing, is back from the wedding and looking for someone to run Titles."

"Is Shelley staying on at Monarch's?" Lee asked.

"Yep. She's officially engaged to Peter as of last week."

"I guess you had to be there," Adam said, looking lost.

Lee laughed. "You sort of did. The Square has had a booming romance thing going on the last few years. We topped it off last summer with a triple wedding. Parker, the princess, and Jace, the private investigator her father hired. Her friend Shey fell in love with Parker's supposed prince fiancé, and their friend Cara fell for Parker's brother, the future king."

"And don't forget Pearly," Juliet added with a sigh. "She went to Europe for the wedding and rediscovered her first love, Buster. He just got back to the States last month and the two of them are on cloud nine."

"Royalty in Erie?" Adam asked. "There hasn't been any mention of that in the paper."

"The paper has stayed hands-off the story, so we all know, but—"

"But it's a secret," Juliet finished.

"The most public secret in Perry Square's history," Lee assured him.

Adam laughed. "So, you're taking me to dine with royalty?"

Lee shrugged and grinned. "Hey, what can I say? Erie's got it all."

"Yes, Erie definitely has a lot going for it." As he said the words he shot Lee a look that made her heart speed up and her temperature kick up a few degrees in a way that had nothing to do with the warm early-summer day.

* * *

Monarch's was a bustling hive of activity. The coffeehouse's tables were all filled and there was a short line at the counter. The glass deli case was filled with sandwiches and salads. There was a soda machine at one end, and a dozen thermal coffee carafes lined a small station next to it.

But Lee's focus wasn't on what type of sandwich she wanted. She was too busy eying the lunchtime crowd nervously. Bringing Adam here might have been a big mistake. "Why don't we get our lunches to go? I mean, we'd have to wait for a table, and last time I was at the zoo, they had a great area for picnicking."

Yes, eating with the animals was preferable to eating with the women who even now eyed Adam as if he were a tasty treat.

Pearly was bad enough, but if Josie and Mabel got their hands on him, even Libby, who was standing with them and would probably try to run interference, wouldn't be able to save her.

Even as she was thinking it, the trio left their place in line and came back to where Lee, Adam and Jessie waited.

Josie was the big-haired redhead manicurist at Snips and Snaps, the beauty shop Libby owned and Pearly worked at. Mabel was the neighborhood manicurist.

"Uh, ho," was all the warning she had time for before they reached them.

"What…?" Adam started, but then he tracked where Lee was looking.

"Now, who is this?" Mabel asked no one in particular.

Josie snapped her gum and smiled. "I'm betting you're Adam." Before Adam could respond, Josie continued, "Pearly told us Lee had a man living with her."

"Next to me," Lee felt compelled to correct.

"And this must be Jessie," Josie said, ignoring Lee.

Libby, the youngest of the trio by at least a decade, laughed. "Sorry. I tried to stop them."

"Thanks." Lee remembered her manners, said, "Adam, this is Mabel, Josie and Libby. They all work on the Square. Ladies, Josie was right, this is Adam Benton and his niece Jessie. They're renting my other cottage."

"Renting your cottage?" Josie repeated. "Is that what they call it these days?"

Mabel snorted, and Lee could tell Libby was trying to look stern, but the small smile that played at the corners of her mouth ruined the effect.

"Next," Parker called.

"That's us." Lee felt a sense of relief. She turned from her curious neighbors and smiled at Perry Square's personal princess, although the tall blonde looked more like a college student in her jeans and T-shirt, than royalty.

"Tuna on whole wheat, for me. Adam?"

"That sounds great."

"Got it," Parker said. But rather than get the sandwiches, she smiled in Adam's direction. He was holding Jessie. "Hi, Adam. I've heard a lot about you. And this is?"

"Jessie," he said. "And just what have you heard?"

"You're living with Lee—"

"Renting my cottage," she corrected.

"And you're here for a month. You brought your niece with you, and you work in New York."

"How—?" he started to ask.

Lee interrupted. "Don't bother asking. The Square has its ways. And of course the fact Parker's married to a private investigator means she's got more ways than others."

Parker laughed as she handed over a bag with the sandwiches. "Picnic?"

"We're taking Jessie to the zoo."

"So, you're dating now?" Mabel asked from behind them.

Lee had almost forgotten them in the face of Parker's curiosity. She realized that they were surrounded. Time to make a break for it. "Well, ladies, Parker, we've got to go."

"Have fun," Parker said.

"And don't do anything I wouldn't do," Josie added.

"That leaves the door wide open," Mabel teased.

"Run," Libby stage-whispered.

Lee, hurrying Adam and Jessie in front of her, was happy to oblige.

* * *

Adam was still chuckling over the coffeeshop interrogation two hours later as they sat in a quiet corner of the zoo.

Lee glared at him. "It wasn't that funny."

"It was."

"You should be horrified by the inquisition. And I don't think either of us mentioned that you were from New York, which probably means Parker had her husband, Jace, check you out."

Adam knew he should be upset by the thought, but he just couldn't manage it. He liked that Lee had so many people looking after her, but she was too busy stewing about the incident to hear that, so he opted to change the subject.

"I think Jessie enjoyed herself." His cousin was sound asleep in her stroller, clutching the stuffed baby orangutan that Lee had insisted on buying her.

"Yes, I think she did. Isn't the zoo great? They've done so many things the last few years. The Children's Zoo, and the new Asian exhibit, and…"

Adam listened as Lee rhapsodized over the zoo's improvements and smiled. There was something about her. Whether she was sitting by herself, quietly watching the lake, or surrounded by friends whose concern flustered her, or holding Jessie… there was something that touched him. Something that called to him.

He'd felt it all those years ago. But now, the feeling was different.

He realized the bench was much too wide for his liking and slid a little closer to Lee. He felt the distinct need to touch her. Well, if he was honest, more than just touch.

"Lee, I—" At that moment, his cellphone rang, which startled Jessie from her light nap.

Lee practically jumped from the bench. "You get that, and I'll get Jessie."

Adam, annoyed by the interruption, answered the phone, "Hello?"

But even as he listened, he watched Lee raise Jessie out of the stroller and the warm feeling spread through his system again.

Yes, there was something between them and somehow he planned to find a way to explore what it was.

As they drove toward the cottages hours later, Adam's cell phone rang for the umpteenth time.

Lee didn't mean to eavesdrop, but there was no way to avoid it. It was obviously yet another business call.

Lee couldn't quite shake memories of her ex. It had haunted her all day.

Alan had also carried his cell with him everywhere. She couldn't remember a time when their evenings and weekends hadn't been interrupted by calls. Business came first. That was Alan's motto.

He'd claimed that he worked so hard for her, for their future, and she'd bought it at first, but soon she'd come to realize that he worked so hard to satisfy some inner sense of ambition and drive. Lee couldn't live that way, and he couldn't curb his workaholism. It was just one of the reasons why they should never have been together. One of the reasons they'd eventually grown apart.

As Adam drove past a vineyard, Lee took in the view, just as she always did. She glanced at Adam and he didn't seem to notice how breathtaking the grapevines were against the backdrop of the lake. His concentration was centered on the road and the conversation in his ear, just as it had been three times during lunch.

"Okay, we'll finish tomorrow." He pulled the earphone out, then turned to Lee and grinned. "We're almost there."

"Yes, we are." She turned back toward her door and stared out the window.

"Hey, did I do something?"

Adam sounded genuinely confused and Lee pushed her annoyance away. After all, he wasn't her ex. This wasn't a date. He was an old friend who was renting her cottage for a month. He had every right to deal with business on a Sunday.

She turned back to him and smiled. "No, you didn't do anything. I was just distracted by how beautiful everything is here in the early summer.

We're beyond that early spring come-to-life period and entering into a season of establishment. Things are growing, the water's warming. Everything's just perfect."

He didn't respond to her little, semi-embarrassing monologue, as he pulled off the main road onto the small dirt road that wound down to the twin cottages. Lee was thankful. She really loved the lake, especially during the summer, but she didn't normally rhapsodize about it like that.

As they approached the cottages, her perfect worldview died in a fatal burst. She groaned as she spied the giant RV parked just behind her cottage. She might have been confused as to who the owners were, if they hadn't been sitting on her porch chairs.

"What are they doing here?" she muttered. "And what on earth are they doing with an RV?"

"Company?" Adam asked.

"My parents."

"I don't really remember them from when I was younger," he mused.

No, he wouldn't remember them.

It had been her grandmother who'd cared for her, spent time with her—it had been her grandmother's house she went to after school each day. Her official address might have been at her parent's house in Erie proper, but her grandmother's cottage was her home. While her mom and dad were putting in the long hours required to build a business from scratch, her grandmother had pretty much raised her.

Her parents waved and started toward the SUV as Adam parked it in front of his cottage.

"Hi, honey," her mother called in a too-jovial sort of tone that made Lee suddenly nervous.

"What are you two doing here?" she asked, and then realized how inhospitable she sounded. To ease the sting, she stepped forward and hugged her mom, then her father.

Before her mother answered her first question, Lee couldn't help asking a second question. "And what on earth are you doing with an RV?"

"An *RV?*" her father parroted. "This isn't just an RV. It's a Coachmen Elite. The outside color is called Copper Mist. Inside there are cherry cabinets, two flat-screen televisions, a full bath, a queen bed in the master bedroom, and a pullout up front. We've even got our sedan hitched to it at the back. It—"

Her mother interrupted him. "Your father's a little excited. I don't think she needs a recap of the features, dear. And to answer your question, we've got an RV because we retired. We're going to spend some time touring the country," her mother said heartily. Too heartily. "You're our first stop."

"Well, congratulations," Lee said, not knowing what else to say to the shocking news.

Her parents…retired?

She never considered they'd leave work behind. Not ever. Their business was everything to them.

They'd started a small accounting firm here in Erie, and merged with a statewide firm, moving to Philadelphia ten years ago, just after Lee had graduated from high school. Oh, they'd visited Erie frequently to check on the branch here…and check on Lee.

But retired?

"What about the firm?"

"We let the partners buy us out," her mother said.

Lee noticed that her father, who might have been a salesman for Coachmen Recreational Vehicles when describing his new toy, wasn't saying much of anything about his retirement, and she wondered what that meant. But she didn't press. She simply said, "So you retired, then you bought an RV."

"And here we are," her mother concluded. Then looked beyond Lee's shoulder.

Lee turned and saw Adam and Jessie there.

"Oh, I'm so sorry. Adam, this is my mother and father, Margaret and Aston Singer. Mom and Dad, Adam Benton and this is Jessie."

Hand shaking and pleased-to-meet-yous gave Lee a moment to gather herself. Her parents had retired and come to visit. It was a lot to take in.

"Want a tour?" her father asked.

It was obvious he wanted her to want a tour, so she smiled and replied, "I'd love one."

Her dad was in heaven as he described all the whosits and whatsits of her parents' new home away from home.

Lee had to admit, the RV was far more spacious than she would have imagined, and the interior decor was beautiful.

As the tour wound down, she asked her most pressing question. "So, how long are you staying?"

"Indefinitely," answered her father.

"How long is indefinitely?" Adam asked later that evening.

Lee jumped at the sound of his voice interrupting the still of the night. She was sitting on her porch trying to sort out the recent turn of events. "I'm going to have to bell the cat or the neighbor in your case."

He laughed. "I don't think I'm all that quiet. You just tend to come out here at night and get lost."

He was right. Gazing out at the evening sky and the pitch blackness that was the lake was enough to settle her mind and allow her to sleep most evenings.

But not tonight.

"Wow," Adam said. "You're not talking. Was dinner with your parents that bad?"

"Let's just say, lunch with you and Jessie was better, even with all your cell phone interruptions."

"I don't know if I should ask what happened with your parents, or apologize for the interruptions. Normally I do have the weekends off, but with being away, things at the office are crazy, hence all the calls. I think I'll just settle for both. I'm sorry, and what happened?"

Lee felt guilty. "I shouldn't have complained about the phone. It really wasn't my place. It's just you reminded me of my ex and…well, now I'm apologizing. Like I said, it wasn't my place. As for dinner with the parents, it was pretty much same old, same old. 'Honey, we're so happy to see you. How's work…if you can call playing with trinkets work.' Blah, blah, blah is pretty much what I hear anymore. Now that Dad has spare time, he went ahead and developed a five-year plan that would make Singer's Treasures bigger and better. 'A real success, dear.'" She had the imitation of her parents down to a T, she realized.

"They don't see that what you do isn't playing, it's art? I saw that when I visited…. The shop is special. Your work is amazing."

"No, that's not what they see. They see wasted potential. I have a degree in art, and I minored in business. After they realized that I wasn't interested in pursuing the business end of things, they'd hoped I'd work at some upscale gallery, something they could brag about." Sometimes she felt as if all her parents had ever been after were bragging rights.

When she was younger, they'd introduce her to friends, then proceed to talk about her straight *As*, or her success on the track team.

They seemed to feel her small Perry Square shop didn't have any brag-ability. She felt as if all their prodding was their attempt to get it back.

"So, instead of me managing an upscale gallery or working at the Smithsonian, all they have to share with friends is my small shop on the Square. I don't think Singer's Treasures measures up to their expectation. I mean, it pays the bills, but it's never going to make me rich. I have can Juliet's salary, pay expenses and support myself in the way I want to live. That's not good enough for them."

That was true, but what she didn't say was that it wasn't just that she didn't think her *business* was good enough for them, she was pretty sure *she* wasn't good enough.

On the other hand, though her parents had done their normal make-your-business-more-of-a-success talk, it hadn't been the driving force of the discussion. They talked enthusiastically about their RV and their plans. They'd asked about Adam. Even asked if Lee was dating, what she was doing for fun. Those personal inquiries were so unlike them.

Adam brushed her arm, calling her attention back to him. "I'm sorry."

"Seems like that's been our refrain tonight." She tried to laugh, but it came out sort of hollow to her own ears. "Really, I'm used to my parents. There are some things in life you just have to get over. I know they love me, and truly, I love them, but we're different. I have different goals than they do, different priorities. They're never going to accept me the way

I am, and I'm never going to change just for their benefit. It's a stalemate."

"Still…"

She leaned up and kissed his cheek. "You don't have to try and make it better. Sometimes it's just nice to have a friendly shoulder."

"Don't let your parents or anyone make you feel like you should apologize for your work, Lee. And knowing what you want and making it happen… that's rare."

"What do you want, Adam? We've talked about my store, my goals, my parents. But what about you? You and Jessie."

"That's what I'm here to find out. What I want. No, not really what I want. What's best for Jessie. That's what it boils down to. And I've got the rest of the month to work it out."

Chapter Four

Monday morning, Adam had watched Lee take off toward the beach at eight. A couple of hours later, she was back at her house. At eleven-thirty, she'd gotten into then out of her Jeep.

He'd wondered off and on all day where she'd gone and what she was doing as he tried to juggle work and Jessie. By late afternoon, Lee still wasn't back. Was she at the shop?

"Not that I'm keeping track," he assured Jessie, who was busy shredding a box of tissues.

He'd thought about taking the tissues away from her, but she was having a great time and, other than a mess, there didn't seem any harm, so he let her go at it. He imagined Lee would have approved.

"Not that I care what Lee thinks."

Jessie blew a raspberry.

"Now, that's just rude," he assured her as the phone rang…again.

He hadn't given much thought to how many calls he received until Lee had mentioned it. This was supposed to be a break so he could figure things out, but he felt as if he were working as hard as ever.

He looked at the caller ID before he answered. "Hi, Darius."

Darius Sheridan was his right-hand man. He was determined to make his own mark on the business and worked harder than anyone Adam knew.

Adam respected that attitude, as much as he enjoyed his friendship with Darius. He'd never have been able to take this leave if it weren't for Darius looking after Delmark.

"How's it going out in the backwoods?" Darius asked.

"Erie's not quite the backwoods." Adam could proclaim that fact until his face turned blue, but he knew Darius believed that any city that wasn't New York was indeed a backwoods.

"It's also not New York," he said, as if on cue. "Speaking of New York…uh, we've got a bit of a glitch I need to talk to you about."

Adam suddenly came to a decision. Something he

hadn't even known he was thinking about. "No. I don't think so."

"Huh?"

Adam recognized Darius's shock at his response. As a matter of fact, he felt a bit of that himself. But Lee's comments still rang in his ears. "Listen, I wouldn't have left you in charge if I didn't trust you. Whatever the glitch is, fix it."

"But—"

"I said call if there was an emergency. A dire emergency. Something you can't handle. I think you can handle almost whatever comes up. Yet, you've called every day—"

"Because it's your company."

"But you're in charge. Now, do you really need me, or can you handle whatever it is?"

There was a long pause. "I can handle it. If you're sure."

"If I hadn't been sure, I wouldn't have left. I need this time, Darius. You need the experience this is giving you. So, if there's a real emergency, something you can't handle, call. Otherwise, I'll check in with you daily, like we planned." Adam hung up.

He sat for a moment, thinking about what he'd just done. He'd started Delmark, Inc. right out of college. He'd been in total control ever since. But he'd just basically handed everything over to Darius.

It should feel scary. His insides should be twisting.

Instead, he realized, it felt good.

Free.

Jessie blew a few spit bubbles, then babbled to herself as she switched from shredding tissues to stacking her plastic multicolored rings.

He looked at his laptop. Even if he'd stemmed the flow of office calls, he still had things he should attend to. He looked back at Jessie.

"Want to get some dinner, squirt?"

She babbled again and he was pretty sure between the *das* and *bas*, there was a yes.

"Well, then let's go. We could ask Lee." He'd noticed her drive off with her father earlier. "Let's see if her parents will help us track her down and we'll find out if she'll join us."

He scooped Jessie up and left the cottage.

Adam realized as he reached the door of the RV and knocked that Jessie was starting to feel at home on his hip. There was an art to properly placing a baby. He'd finally acquired it.

The door swung open, and Adam felt as if he'd somehow been transported back to junior high, showing up on a doorstep to collect a girl for a date.

"Hi, Mrs. Singer. I was wondering if you knew where Lee went? Her car's still in the driveway, but she's not around." Yes, he was indeed reduced to his awkward teen years.

"My daughter went to work today. Her check engine light was coming on, so her father took her in. He tinkered with it and found it was just a clogged air filter."

"Do you know when she's closing the shop today?"

"Since she feels as if working more than six hours on any given day is tantamount to *giving in to the man—*"

Mr. Singer came up behind his wife. "Lee closes the store around five. I'm supposed to pick her up then."

"Jessie and I are heading into town. We could save you a trip and bring her home."

"That won't be necessary," Mrs. Singer assured him.

For a moment, he thought Lee's dad was going to agree with her, but he said, "Thanks. That would be great."

Adam beat a hasty retreat.

Though he knew Lee and Mrs. Singer were mother and daughter, he found the connection amazing. Other than a cursory physical resemblance, he didn't see any similarities between then. Lee was open, always smiling, while her mother had lines on her face that Adam doubted had anything to with laughter.

"Come on, Jessie. How about we head into town for that dinner? You can catch a bit of a nap in the car on the way."

She burbled her agreement as he carried her back

into the house to pack a diaper bag. He grabbed his keys, and automatically reached for his cell phone. For an instant, remembering Lee's words, he was tempted to leave it behind. But despite his talk with Darius, he had responsibilities, so reluctantly he slipped the device into his pocket.

"Come on, Jessie. Let's go."

Lee sat at the back counter and pretended to work, but in actuality, she was praying for some kind of distraction.

A customer.

A phone call.

Heck, even her mom and dad would be welcomed.

She needed something to keep her from her thoughts. Her mind would drift to Adam, then to Jessie. From there her thoughts tripped in directions that tore at her heart. She'd think back, delving into the past and a place she'd hoped she'd put behind her.

As if an answer to a prayer, Pearly Gates waltzed into the shop. "A bunch of us are going over to the Five and Dine for dinner. You interested?"

"I don't know. I probably should—"

"They have potato soup today."

"You're not playing fair." The Five and Dine's potato soup was out of this world.

"And rumor has it the soup comes with garlic bread. You know how theirs is always so crispy around the edges, but soft in the middle. It practically melts in your mouth."

Well, she'd been hoping for a distraction, and dinner would certainly qualify. "I'm in."

"Good, we'll—" Pearly cut herself off when Adam opened the door and tried to hold it wide while pushing the stroller through.

"Here, let me help," Pearly said, propping the door for him.

"Thanks. You'd think there was a better system for this," he grumbled as he wheeled in. He grinned at Lee. "We ran out of tissues."

She must have looked puzzled, because he added, "Jessie's decided de-rolling toilet paper isn't nearly as fascinating as shredding tissues. But we're out, so we're off to buy more. And as long as we're in town, we thought we'd see if you'd like to get dinner."

"I'm sorry. I just made plans with—"

"What's one more? Well, one and a half." Pearly mussed Jessie's wispy hair. "I'm sure I speak for everyone when I say, the more the merrier."

Before Lee could offer up some excuse, Adam said, "As long as you don't mind, Jessie and I would be delighted to join you."

"Tell you what, Lee," Pearly said. "You just take your time closing up the shop and I'll meander over to the Five and Dine with Adam here."

"You know my name?" Adam said, as he was practically herded, stroller and all, out the door by Pearly.

"I know about everythin' that happens here on the Square," Pearly said. "It's a gift. Sort of like my great-uncle Josiah Gates. Why he…"

As Pearly helped Adam maneuver the stroller back through the door, he cast Lee a final help-me look.

Lee might have found the situation amusing, but she knew that Pearly was going to pump Adam for information. And she knew from past experience that before this dinner was over, Pearly would know all the pertinent, and probably not so pertinent, facts about Mr. Adam Mathias Benton.

That's why she was hurrying to close up the shop. Out of a feeling of loyalty to her old school friend.

Okay, school nemesis. But even nemeses formed bonds, and it was up to her to save Adam.

She closed the register, counted the drawer, prepared the day's deposit and was just about ready to make her getaway and ride to Adam's rescue, when the door opened and Mrs. Ramsey came in. "Lee, dear, I'm so glad you're still here. I need a present for tonight…"

Part of Lee wanted to tell Mrs. Ramsey that the store was closed, but her mother's latest lecture was still ringing in her ears, so she forced herself to do the responsible thing and say, "What did you have in mind?"

"That was…" Adam paused, looking for a word, and finally settled on saying, "Interesting," as they drove back toward the cottages.

Lee laughed. "I should have warned you, but Pearly had you out the door and headed across the park before I could get a word out edgewise."

"I imagined meeting a few of your friends again. A *quiet*, intimate dinner."

"When Perry Square gets together it's always more than a few. But hey, at least this was just a small get-together. You should see them when they have a real all-out bash."

"There's more?" In Adam's opinion, there had been enough Perry Square residents to fill most of the Five and Dine, and all of them had felt the need to look out for Lee, which meant finding out about him.

"Yes. Lots more."

"And do they all consider you a surrogate daughter, sister, or simply a friend?" he asked.

"I'd like to think so."

"Well, let's just say, your parents didn't grill me that hard. As a matter of fact, they haven't grilled me at all." He laughed.

Lee tried to join him, but couldn't quite muster up any humor. "My mother and father aren't the grilling type. To be honest, I don't remember them ever checking out a man I was seeing." She paused.

He glanced over, and she was blushing.

"Not that we're seeing each other," she added quickly.

Part of Adam wanted to argue, but he chose not

to say anything mainly because he wasn't sure what to say.

He hadn't come to Erie to date anyone. He didn't have the time and definitely had more than enough on his plate right now with the baby and the business. But despite his best intentions, he thought there was a very good possibility he'd inadvertently added Lee to the mix.

They rode in silence for a while, and finally Lee said, "Would it be awful if I confess that I don't want to go home just yet?"

"Because of your parents?" There was something there, between the three of them. Listening to Lee's comments, he could feel it. Having watched them all together, he sensed a formality, and maybe a nervousness.

"I love them," Lee said. "Really, I do. But…"

"They make it hard."

She nodded. "Listen, I know how lucky I am. Truly. I have friends who can't stand their parents and vice versa. I love mine, and I know they love me. The kind of love that would do anything. If I needed blood, they'd slit open their wrists to give it to me without a second thought. But while they were at it, they'd lecture me about how irresponsible I was to lose my own blood and need theirs."

Adam tried to hold it back—Lee could see how valiantly he fought—but in the end, he lost and chuckled.

"It's not funny," she protested, but even as the words came out of her mouth, she started to chuckle, too. "Okay, so maybe I was a bit melodramatic."

"I could see the picture you painted. Having met your parents, I can really see it in my head."

"Like I said, I love them, but sometimes it's hard to remember that I do."

"Like when their RV's parked in your driveway, next to your cabin?"

"Especially then. Or when they start on yet another one of their you're-wasting-your-life lectures."

"Well, I can't fix all that, but I can make the evening last longer," Adam offered. "Go for a drive. If I remember correctly, there's that small public beach in North East—"

"Freeport," she supplied.

"Yes. We could take a walk there and look for more of your beach glass."

"You wouldn't mind? I mean, you don't have work you have to do?"

"A very wise person pointed out that maybe I work too much. Did you notice not one cell phone call during dinner?"

"I'll confess, I did."

He glanced over again and she was smiling. "I told my replacement to deal with the current crisis, and came to find you."

"I'm glad you did find me…and the rest as well. Life is meant to be enjoyed."

"Well, I plan on enjoying an evening walking along the lake with you and Jessie."

It turned out that Jessie preferred walking in the water, to along the shore.

As they walked, Lee realized that there was something different about tonight, as she took a turn carrying the rather soggy Jessie.

She glanced at Adam, who was diligently studying the sand, watching for the brief sparkle of the sun's last rays catching a piece of glass.

So earnest and intent.

It touched her.

Most of her walks were solitary ones. She suddenly realized how much time she had spent by herself the last year.

More than that.

Even when she'd been married to Alan, he'd traveled a lot, so she'd been on her own more often than not.

She was lucky though, she had friends on the Square. She went out to lunches and dinners, even attended the occasional party. But the majority of her time she spent in her own company.

Until this moment, that was the way she'd liked it. She'd appreciated being by herself with her thoughts. But she had to confess, there was something that felt right about walking with Adam and Jessie. They weren't talking, just sharing the experience.

At that moment, Jessie tried to dive out of her arms and back into the water. Lee held on and laughed. "No more swimming tonight.

Adam looked and their eyes met. He offered her a slow, lazy smile. And the sight, all the time she'd spent alone didn't feel so comfortable.

It felt…lonely.

She realized that when the month was over and Adam left, she'd miss him. She'd miss this. It really was ridiculous. They hadn't been very close friends when they were young, and now he'd only been in Erie a handful of days. But even knowing that it didn't make sense, she knew the feeling was real.

She'd miss him when he was gone.

She reached out and touched Jessie's hair, laughing as the toddler continued to squirm and tried to break free.

"I almost had a baby once just like you." She realized she'd said the words out loud, and turned away, ready to hurry back to the car.

Why on earth had she said that?

Maybe Adam hadn't noticed.

She didn't look at him to see if he had. Even if he'd heard her, maybe he'd just let it go? But he touched her arm and Lee knew he knew.

Lee froze as he took Jessie from her arms and sat the toddler on the ground. Jessie squealed with laughter.

"Tell me," he asked, simply. He pulled her down

onto the sand. They sat, side by side, almost touching, but not quite.

"I didn't mean to say that. I don't know why I did. I never talk about…" She just let the sentence die.

"Maybe you said it because you never talk about it. Tell me. I'd like to know."

Lee drew in a deep breath, and tried to sort out where to start.

The sun was slipping, almost touching the water now. Jessie was picking up small stones and tossing them.

Lee concentrated on the toddler, rather than look at Adam as she began. "I married right out of college. Alan was older. He was an established businessman by the time I graduated. Driven to make something of himself. And me? I was naive. I thought our marriage would be different than our dating and engagement were, and it was. It was worse. I hardly ever saw him. He traveled much of the time, and when he was in town he worked impossibly long hours. I guess I hadn't noticed as much when I was in school because there was always so much going on. But after we were married, I did…boy, did I notice. When we decided to start a family and I got pregnant, again I naively thought maybe he'd change."

There. The sun was touching the water now.

Lee knew from years of experience that it would quickly slide beneath the horizon. Pink and orange tinged the lower edge of the sky as the lake seemingly swallowed up the sun. The color backlit Jessie, and Lee wished she'd brought a camera so she could capture this moment.

"But he didn't change?" Adam asked softly.

Lee shook her head. Bit by bit, the sun was disappearing, blazing a final color display in its wake.

"What happened?"

"I was six months along. I could feel the baby move and kick. I'd sit for hours trying to decide if a particular bulge was an arm, or maybe a little foot. The night I started bleeding, Alan was in Chicago. I called 911. The whole trip to the hospital, I kept calling him, but by the time he got my message it was over. We'd lost our baby girl."

Adam draped an arm on her shoulder. "I'm sorry."

She finally looked at him. She could see empathy in his eyes as he tightened his arm around her.

When she'd lost the baby, there had been no one to hold her like this. No one to lean on. It hadn't even occurred to her to call her parents until the next morning.

Her mother had come right away, arriving before Alan, but she'd looked uncomfortable when Lee had started to talk about her baby and her sense of loss, so she'd stopped.

When Alan had come, he'd said the right words, but she'd found it hard to forgive him for not being there.

It would be easy to blame her marriage's failure on losing the baby, but afterward, she'd realized her marriage had stopped working a long time before they'd lost their daughter.

Sometimes she'd wondered if it ever really had worked at all.

"Lee," Adam said. Just her name. But there was a world of concern infused in it.

"I try and tell myself it was probably for the best. They say you learn your parenting skills from your parents, and if that's the case, it's best history does not repeat itself."

"Your parents were that bad?" he asked.

"No," she said, honestly. "They were just that disinterested. Like Alan, they lived for ambition, for getting ahead."

"But you're not like that."

"Maybe. I mean, I don't live to work. But I'm selfish in my own way. I like having time for myself, for my art," she confessed, voicing her worry for the first time. "I don't fool myself that I'm a Picasso, but I love creating things. It's different than being driven in the business world, but maybe my needs would eventually supercede the baby's needs. And I truly believe you shouldn't have children unless you can put them first. I don't know that I'd be able to do that, so it's best I don't have any."

"At least that's what you tell yourself."

His insight surprised her, but she found herself nodding. "Yes. It makes the pain a little more tolerable…sometimes."

At that moment a wave swept near Jessie and she went over. Both Adam and Lee jumped up, but before they could pull Jessie up, the toddler righted herself, giggling as she smacked the sand.

Laughing as well, Adam lifted the more than slightly soggy little girl. "Time to head home."

Placing Jessie on his hip, he held her with one arm, reached out with the other and took Lee's hand. He gave it the slightest squeeze.

As Lee looked up at him, she realized how much things had changed. She wasn't sure to what extent but, at the moment, she didn't want to analyze it. She simply held Adam's hand and walked toward the car listening to Jessie gurgle.

And she realized, at this moment in time, she wasn't lonely at all.

Chapter Five

"We're here," Adam said, a half hour later as he cut the engine in front of the cottages.

Lee turned around and glanced at Jessie. "She's conked out in her car seat."

He glanced back. Sure enough, the baby's head lolled to the side as she slept.

They'd stripped her wet clothes off, put on a fresh diaper and a T-shirt that he'd had the foresight to keep in the diaper bag. Her hair, still baby-fine, had long since dried.

Looking at Jessie, something twisted in his heart.

"She had a good day." That's what he wanted for her, a lifetime of good days. He still wasn't any closer to deciding if he'd be the best one to give her those, or if her grandparents were.

That's what Jessie deserved…the best.

A childhood of happy days.

As if reading his thoughts, Lee asked, "Have you made any decisions?"

"No. I know that Paul and Cathie wanted me to raise her, but…"

He let the sentence die.

But.

There were a myriad of *buts*.

But he had his business.

But he had his baby-free life.

But—the biggest but—he wasn't sure he could do it.

He thought about what Lee had said.…Parents had to put their children first. Maybe he was too selfish to do that.

He'd built Delmark from scratch. Now with Darius onboard, the company was ready to expand into an entirely new market.

Could he put aside his myopic focus from his business and shift it to Jessie?

Again, it was as if Lee read his mind. "But you worry you won't be a good enough parent."

That was the biggest *but* of all. "Yes."

"I understand."

The wonderful thing was, he knew she did. He

felt connected to someone, aligned with someone, for the first time that he could remember.

Lee took his hand and patted it. Just a small comforting touch. A touch that left him wanting more.

She understood, and didn't demure, but simply slid closer and moved into his embrace.

There was no explosion as they kissed, just a gentle connection. Soft, inviting, comforting—it tugged at him, pulling him toward her, prompting him to deepen the kiss.

Again, Lee met him halfway and joined him.

His hands slid to her shirt, pulling it from her waistband. He caressed her bare stomach, sliding his hand higher, higher—

A bright light flooded the car.

"What the—"

Lee pulled away and straightened her shirt. "My parents."

"They're flashing a light on us?" he asked, amusement overriding his feelings of frustration.

"Are you having high-school flashbacks all of a sudden, or what?" she asked, laughing.

He turned. "They're standing outside the RV, looking our way. And they don't look as if they're going to go in until we come out."

Just then, Jessie stirred in the back and started whining.

"Sounds like our quiet time is over anyway."

"Maybe we can pick things up again later, when Jessie and your parents are asleep?"

"I could sneak over with a bottle of wine."

"Well, at least this isn't high school and you don't have to climb out the window."

"No. Not quite. I think it's time I had a chat with my parents—set some ground rules for this visit. And you should probably go bathe Jessie. I think she brought half the beach home in her hair."

"Later then?" he asked.

"Later." Lee watched Adam unbuckle Jessie from her car seat and bundle her into the house before turning her attention to her parents, who still stood outside the RV.

Taking a deep, calming breath, she walked over to them.

"What was that all about?" she asked as she approached them.

"We decided to step outside and look at the stars, so we turned on the light," her mother said innocently.

"Ha."

"Fine. It's unseemly for a woman your age to be parked in a car, making out with a man."

"First, I think it's important to remember that this is my home, my driveway, and I can park with whomever I want. I'm certainly of age. But even if I weren't, you wouldn't have any right to stop me."

"I'm your mother. It's my job to stop you from making foolish mistakes—to worry about you."

"Really?"

Most of the time Lee was able to put aside childhood resentments and accept her parents as they were. But every now and then, the feelings bubbled to the surface. "It seems like a strange time to remember that fact. It might have meant something when I was in grade school, or even high school, but now, it's too late. Don't try to pretend you worry—that I matter. Just because you're at loose ends and not sure what to do without the business, that doesn't mean you can barge into my life and try to keep yourself busy by pretending you care."

"Lee…"

Her mother didn't say anything else. Part of Lee wished she'd say, *We love you. I love you. We're sorry we ignored you all those years. Let us make it up to you now.* And part of Lee knew she wouldn't know what to say in return. So maybe she was lucky her mother didn't say any of those things. She simply turned around and walked back into the RV.

That was fine with Lee. It wasn't as if she expected any great mother-daughter moment.

She turned and went back into her cottage, trying to ignore the hollow feeling in her chest. She'd spent years tamping down feelings of neglect, of being ignored. She tried to pretend coming in a distant second to her parents' work schedule didn't bother her.

But sometimes pretending didn't work and the

feelings spewed over and she found herself saying things she knew had hurt her mother.

She banged around in her kitchen, looking for a bottle of wine she knew she'd bought a few months ago, but couldn't remember where she'd put it.

Finally she found it under the sink, and hurried out of the cottage toward Adam's.

She wanted to be held.

She wanted to tell him about what she'd said and have him understand. She wanted him to tell her she had to go apologize tomorrow, because as much as she knew she should, part of her had wanted to say those words for so long. Apologizing for them would be hard, even though she knew she had to.

She knocked softly on his door.

There was no answer.

Maybe he was putting Jessie into bed.

She opened the door and let herself in, expecting the living room to be empty.

Instead, she saw Adam in the rocking chair holding Jessie, both of them sound asleep.

She wasn't sure how long she stood there simply drinking in the sight, but somewhere along the line, the change that she had felt earlier began to shift a bit. She realized that she felt more than an old kinship with Adam. More than a simple camaraderie.

She felt something much richer and deeper.

A feeling that scared her.

Adam was a businessman. She'd been there and done that. First her parents, then her ex. Lee tried not to repeat her mistakes.

And Adam would be a mistake. She had to remember that. Because if she forgot, she just might fall in love with him. And she knew that loving a man who put business first and her second again would break her heart.

Chapter Six

A baby was crying. But Lee ignored everything except work....

Lee sat in Singer's Treasures trying to shake the vestiges of last night's dream, but she could still hear the echoes of her baby's cry in her head as she worked on the small pin.

It felt as if the quiet life she'd so carefully constructed was unraveling bit by bit.

She'd wondered if her parents would still be parked next to her cottage the morning after her fight with her mother, but they were. They'd come over for lunch. Her mother had seemed willing to pretend that the previous night's confrontation hadn't happened, and Lee had obliged.

That was how it had always been with her parents…pretending they had a good relationship, when in actuality they didn't have any relationship outside of the biological connection.

Adam had been buried in work. He'd said something about a crisis that he'd thought he could delegate and in the end couldn't. Lee actually welcomed the bit of distance this gave her. It made it easier to put her rampaging feelings back in check.

She'd spent the afternoon watching Jessie for him.

The toddler was a joy. Even her mother and father seemed to fall under Jessie's spell. The little girl gave them a bridge to their pretense.

But today, sitting in the shop, there was no Jessie to occupy, no uncomfortable strain between Lee and her parents. No customers to speak of.

There was just a lot of quiet and even more thoughts banging around in her head. Whenever she thought about Adam, she felt buoyed and bubbly. But then when she remembered he was leaving in just under three weeks, a heavy weight settled in her stomach, pulling her back down to earth with a thud.

Round and round her thoughts and emotions spun.

Pearly Gates waltzed into the shop and the spinning stopped immediately.

"We all liked your beau," she announced with no preamble. She took the stool on the other side of the display case.

"I'm glad you liked Adam." Lee liked him as

well, not that she was going to go around advertising just how much.

She realized she'd better nip Pearly's gaga expression in the bud. "And, for the record, he's not my beau."

"I know I'm not hip. What do you call a beau these days. Your guy? Your fella? Your significant other?"

"None of the above. Adam's just someone I used to know. Someone who's renting my cottage for a few more weeks." If he was staying…if he wasn't a workaholic, could it be more?

"Those are logical reasons not to have a relationship. But logic doesn't come into play when the heart's concerned," Pearly said softly. "Take it from someone who knows. Buster and I lived two very different lives, and yet…"

"That *and yet*. I'm well acquainted with it, Pearly. Despite all my very valid reasons not to, I'm falling," Lee said simply. It felt good to admit it. "I don't know why, don't know what to do about it."

Pearly just smiled an I-knew-it-all-the-time sort of smile.

"I have all the symptoms," Lee continued. "When I'm not with him, I wish I was. And when we're together, I don't ever want to leave."

"Good for you," the gray-haired beautician said, grinning from ear to ear.

"No. Not so good for me." The leaden feeling

was back in the pit of Lee's stomach. "He's only here for a month, then he's heading back to New York, and back to work."

"You say *work* like it's a four-letter word."

"It is a four-letter word," Lee felt obliged to point out.

Pearly laughed. "Yes, I guess it is at that. But for some people, it's a calling. Take me, for instance. I like cutting hair, and I'm good at it. I like that I get to chat with people, to hear their stories—"

"And telling yours."

Pearly didn't seem to take offense. "Yes. And tellin' mine. There's an art to finding just the right story for the right problem. Now, there's the story of me and Buster. How we let pride and misunderstandings get in the way of our love, and wasted all kinds of precious years. It's a good story, but it wouldn't work for your problem."

Lee had seen Pearly and Buster, and knew that there was a happy ending in the making there.

"But," Pearly continued, "maybe if you look at another aspect of our story, it would. We may have come from the same town, but we've lived our lives in two different worlds. Two very different worlds. One of his best friends is a king, for goodness sakes."

"One of your friends is a princess," Lee pointed out. "Actually, now that Cara and Shey are married to princes, you could say three of your friends are princesses. Doesn't three princesses beat one king?"

"We're not talking poker, we're talking about you and your beau. You do see work as a four-letter word. Sittin' in this shop, day after day, would drive you insane. You're an artist."

Lee felt a familiar wave of discomfort. "Not an artist. That sounds too…I don't know, presumptuous. I just make jewelry."

"There's no *just* to anything you do, girl. And sitting in a building all day, every day, would stifle your artistic heart. You're not a nine-to-fiver. It's not in your makeup. What you don't seem to understand is some people thrive in an office as much as you blossom on the beach, in the open. I had a cousin, Jon."

"Jon?" Lee teased, hoping to distract Pearly from the lecture. "Not *Lerlene,* or *Fancy Mae*. Just a plain name like *Jon?*"

"Well, Jon's last name was Hasenhuettl, so I figure his mama thought a name like Hasenhuettl was enough of a burden for anyone to bear. I mean, teachin' a child to write that name?"

Lee thought she'd managed to get Pearly off on a tangent, which was good. Pearly's perception hit too close to home sometimes. This was one of those times. "I see your point. But still, *Jon*. It's a plain name. Now *Lerlene,* that's a name. Didn't she marry a man who lost his leg?"

"No, but she was engaged to him." Pearly laughed. "And as much as that's a good story as well, it's not the one you're needin' today. You need to hear about Jon. He started a recycling plant. Picking through junk doesn't sound like a job I'd enjoy, but Jon, he found a way to help save the planet, and huggin' trees meant something for him. So going to work each day was a joy for him, just as much as walking on a beach is for you. Everyone has their own gifts, their own callings. Don't you be forgetting that. For me, it's hair and storytelling...." She paused a moment, then said, "This is where you agree."

"Oh, sorry." Lee could tell she was walking a thin line with Pearly and hastily agreed. "Of course, storytelling is your gift."

When Pearly didn't appear quite satisfied, Lee added, "And hair. You're fantastic with hair."

Pearly looked mollified. "Thanks. Those are my callings. And yours is art. Maybe Adam's gift is business. If it makes him happy and he thrives on it, would you really take it away from him?"

Lee knew Pearly was right. "No."

"Of course, you wouldn't, because his passion for what he does is part of him."

"Tell me, what do I do then? I've found a man I could fall for, but I've been down the relationship road with a workaholic before. I don't want to go down it again. Plus, Adam lives in New York, I live here in Erie."

When Pearly didn't respond, Lee said, "Really. What do I do? You're the lady with all the answers."

"No, I'm the lady with all the stories," Pearly corrected. "The only answers for you aren't with me, they're with you. You have to find them for yourself."

"Pearly, that wasn't overly helpful." Lee realized how much she'd hoped that Pearly would give her something to hold onto. Some plan to ward off her growing feelings for Adam.

"Maybe, maybe not. If you're falling for Adam, and if it's a true enough feeling, you'll just have to find those answers."

The door opened and Josie, Mabel and Libby walked in. "Hi, Lee," Libby said. "Pearly, are you ready?"

"Yes. I was just about to ask Lee if she'd like to join us."

"We're heading to the movies for a chick-flick fest." Josie snapped her gum for emphasis. "You're welcome to join us."

"No. But thanks."

The last thing Lee wanted was to immerse herself in someone else's relationship on the big screen where it always seemed to work out. And she was having a hard time believing in happily-ever-afters at the moment.

Even though she really liked Adam, and could probably cross the line to more than liking, she didn't know if she had the strength and the courage to date another man who was so committed to his work, one who was only visiting Erie short-term. Especially one who came equipped with a baby.

But as she thought about Jessie, the familiar ache didn't stab with its same intensity. In the two years since she'd lost her baby, Lee had become accustomed to that pain. For so long seeing any baby had been like ripping off a scab, bringing all the ache and longing back with a force. But spending time with Jessie had been a balm.

Lee realized she didn't see Jessie as a reminder of the baby she'd lost, but simply as a sweet toddler who made her smile. Watching her antics at the beach, at the zoo had simply brought her happiness.

Adam was only here temporarily. He'd leave and go back to his life, and she'd get back to hers, with the addition of some beautiful memories.

Maybe it would be okay. She wouldn't worry about defining what they had. She'd just enjoy it until he left.

Feeling better, she figured she should start acting like it.

"You're sure," asked Mabel, the Square's acupuncturist.

"Yes, I'm sure." Lee felt more settled than she had in a while. "I have other plans. But thanks."

Adam had finally cleared up Delmark's major distribution glitch. An entire week's orders had been lost, and though Darius was competent, he'd needed help smoothing over dozens of customers' ruffled feathers. He'd just hung up the phone with Darius, when it rang again.

"Adam, it's Lee."

"Hi. What's up?"

"I wondered if… Well, I thought maybe you and Jessie might enjoy coming to my place tonight for dinner. We could cook out." She sounded a bit hesitant about the invitation.

"You're sure?" he asked. "Because you don't sound quite sure."

"Yes. I thought it would be fun."

To say he pounced on the invitation would be an understatement. "Well, then we'll be there. What time?"

"When you look out and see the grill going, that's the time."

"I guess it's lucky for me we're neighbors."

She paused again. "Lucky for me as well. See you tonight."

Though he'd been tied up with work, he hadn't been able to stop thinking about her. Thinking about their almost make-out session in his car.

He felt like a kid anticipating Christmas as he made his world-famous potato salad.

Okay, so maybe not world-famous, but certainly the most edible thing in his cooking repertoire. Adam wasn't much use in the kitchen, but this was his specialty dish. One that he could always count on being edible. The trick to a good potato salad was real mayonnaise, lots of hard-boiled eggs and a generous hand with the parsley.

"So, Miss Jess, are you ready?" he asked later that afternoon, shortly after Lee had gotten home.

He'd wanted to run out immediately, but decided to try and play it cool, even if cool was the last thing he felt around Lee Singer.

Jessie drooled her response.

She'd been drooling a lot lately, which, according to the baby books, meant more teeth. She had two front teeth on the bottom, two on the top. And last night he'd caught a flash of white next to those top ones.

Deftly, he wiped the dribble on a spit cloth, tucked the cloth back in the diaper bag, scooped up Jessie in one arm and the potato salad in the other.

He was starting to feel as at home carrying Jessie as he was in his casual attire. Up until this vacation, the only place he'd worn shorts was at the gym. But there was a certain freedom he was beginning to relish in his new wardrobe.

"Let's go see if Lee needs help with the barbecue."

They walked the short distance that spanned the two cottages. Lee was just emerging from hers.

"You're here," she said, a smile on her face.

Her obvious pleasure warmed Adam in a way that had nothing to do with the early evening sun.

"I brought homemade potato salad." He handed the bowl to her.

"Oh, that's great. I have macaroni salad. I'll confess, mine came from the deli." She lifted the bowl's lid. "You really made this?"

"So, now you're a sexist, Mary Eileen? Men can't cook and all that?" he teased.

"No, of course not." She set the bowl on the picnic table along with a number of other dishes and condiments. "I know men who cook. I just didn't imagine you as one of them. You don't have an in-the-kitchen feel about you."

"What kind of feel do I have?" He knew he was blatantly flirting.

Lee didn't seem to mind; in fact, she joined right in. "Well, I would have discovered that the other night, but someone was sleeping instead."

He'd found the bottle of wine on the table next to the door and knew Lee had left it so he'd know she'd been there. He couldn't believe he'd dozed off. "Maybe we could have a replay? I swear I'll stay awake this time."

Lee started, "I—" But Jessie interrupted by giving a gutsy holler, interrupting their flirting.

"How rude of me, ignoring you. Come here, sweetie." Lee held her hands out for the baby.

Jessie readily abandoned Adam and babbled her happiness at Lee.

"Nice. Just steal away my cousin's affections."

"You'll have to take her back while I start the steaks."

"Or, you two ladies could catch up and I could grill them, if you want?"

"Is this nervousness because I said I bought the macaroni salad and you're unsure about my cooking abilities?"

"No, it's just me trying to impress you with my willingness to pitch in."

"You don't need to try to impress me, I already am." Lee looked startled, as if the words had slipped out.

Maybe that's why they felt all the more precious to Adam. "I impress you, eh? I like the sound of that."

"Don't get too puffed up, Benton," she warned. "I'm notoriously fickle. My opinion changes on a dime."

"I don't know. You seemed capable of holding onto your opinion of me when we were young just fine."

"You did pick on me horribly." Jessie started squirming, obviously wanting down. Lee set her on the ground, plucked a wooden spoon off the picnic table and handed it to her.

Jessie was delighted with the improvised toy and started to beat the ground with it.

"All that tormenting was just my way of saying I liked you." He paused and added for good measure, "I've worked out better ways to impress women since then."

"By offering to help cook?"

"Yes. And wooing them with my potato salad."

She laughed. "Fine, you win. Impress me with your barbecuing abilities. Jessie and I will set the picnic table."

Lee plucked up Jessie and turned to head into the cottage, Jessie sitting snugly on her hip. Adam drank in the sight. He liked seeing Lee look so comfortable with the baby, especially after she'd told him about the child she'd lost.

How could her ex leave her alone to cope with something like that?

Adam focused on business as much as the next guy, but he'd drop everything if Jessie needed him. Or Lee.

Mary Eileen Singer meant something to him. He wasn't sure just what it was, or what it could be, but it was there. And it was growing.

She'd already lit the grill. The marinated steaks were sitting on the small table next to it, ready to go. He'd just picked up the tongs when Lee's mother and father rounded the corner of the cottage.

"Yoo-hoo," her mother said brightly. "We thought we smelled the grill and thought we'd bring our hamburgers over here, rather than having to heat up the RV broiling them. It's not exactly spacious and if you light the broiler, it heats the whole place up. You don't mind, do you?"

Adam felt a wave of disappointment. He'd hoped to have Lee all to himself. But just then, Lee came back out, still holding Jessie, along with plates and napkins. At her less-than-enthusiastic expression, her mother's smile faded, and Adam felt a wave of sympathy for them both, so he bit back his disappointment and forced a smile.

"Of course, we don't mind. I was just telling Lee that grilling is a manly pursuit, and was about to show her how it's done. I'd be happy to throw your burgers on as well."

Her mother shot him a look of gratitude. "Great. I've got some baked beans in the oven. I'll run over and get them and we'll have a veritable picnic."

"Great," Lee finally echoed, though the word sounded forced coming from her. "Jessie, come on, sweetie. We'll go get some more plates."

"Let me help you," her father offered.

"That's all right, Dad, maybe you can give Adam a hand with the grilling."

"Glad to see you recognize the manliness of grilling," Adam teased, hoping to ease some of her tension. It seemed to have the desired effect because she smiled, though not as broadly as before. With Jessie still on her hip, she hurried back into the house.

Lee's father walked over to Adam and handed him the plate of hamburgers.

"I'm sorry. We're butting in and I know it, but my wife…" He shook his head. "Well, she's come to the conclusion that Lee needs us and is bound and determined to be here."

"Why does she think Lee needs you?" Adam asked, putting the burgers on the grill next to the steaks.

"You've heard about her ex, about the baby she lost?"

Adam nodded.

Mr. Singer looked surprised. "I guess that's progress. She doesn't talk about either of them normally. It's been two years since she lost the baby. She divorced soon after. Her husband had been gone more than he was present for longer than that. My daughter's always been solitary, but she's been even more so since then. Even to me, she's seemed alone. A little lost. When we retired, my wife decided to fix things. Hence the RV that's parked on the other side of Lee's cottage. But I think rather than fixing things, we're interfering in your relationship."

Relationship? Is that what he had with Lee?

Maybe. Maybe just the beginning of one. But he wouldn't be around long enough to see it come to fruition. He had to remember that.

Had to be sure Lee remembered that.

He was leaving. If things kept spiraling out of control at Delmark, maybe sooner than he'd planned. The last thing he wanted to do was hurt Lee.

He said the words aloud, as a reminder to himself. "I'm only here until the end of the month. What Lee and I have is a friendship. Maybe a little flirting. But nothing that you're interfering with. And even if you were, maybe knowing that someone cares is what she needs, Mr. Singer."

He slapped Adam on the back. "Call me Aston. And thanks."

"So, what do you say we start up the steaks and burgers, Aston?"

The older man smiled. "I say, you're on."

Lee watched her parents and Adam carry on a steady conversation. They talked business, with a casual ease that left her feeling like an outsider.

She was thankful she had Jessie to pay attention to. She'd offered to hold the squirming toddler during dinner, and had ended up with Cheerios serving as her salad's croutons. Finally, convinced Jessie had consumed enough finger foods to keep her going, Lee set her on the ground. The toddler was off like a shot to the stones that lined the path. She seemed content to stack them in small piles.

Unfortunately, Jessie's playing meant Lee had no excuse not to join in the current state-of-the-city discussion.

"We were amazed at all the changes," her mother said. "Of course we've visited, but only a few days here and there. We hadn't really taken in the sights for years."

Adam's cell phone rang. He took it out of his pocket, glanced at the number. "Sorry. I really have to take this."

He got up from the table and moved a short distance away.

Lee's mother picked up where she'd left off. "Why, we were at the peninsula the other day and had a chance to tour the new Visitor's Center. Have you been there yet, Lee?"

"No. Not yet." She desperately tried to think of something to add, but came up blank, so took another bite of potato salad instead.

Adam had been right, he could cook.

She glanced at him, still talking on the phone. It was a déjà vu moment, only back then it would have been her ex on the phone.

She tamped her annoyance down. How Adam handled mixing his work and private life was his own business.

"Well, the Visitor's Center is fantastic."

Lee swallowed the bite and said, "I'm sure it is."

Her mother frowned, obviously hoping for more, but Lee wasn't sure what to make of this newfound parental concern. She didn't know what her mother wanted her to say. "Uh, I'll have to visit soon," she tried.

"So, how's the shop?" her father asked, in an obvious attempt to draw her out.

"It's fine. At least in my opinion. I—" She knew her father had meant to be kind, but this was a sore subject between them. She could have added that she was sure her parents both had suggestions for the shop and changes to her life in general, but she reined them in. Instead, she stood. "Excuse me, I'll go get the dessert."

She practically ran into the house. Why on earth was her first response to her parents to get her back up? Her grandmother had taught her better than that.

Sometimes you just have to accept people the way they are, and realize you can't make them what you want them to be. You can't change them. They have to do it on their own.

Maybe they are, she thought. She'd all but given up hoping they'd see things from her point of view.

Hoping they'd see her, period.

Still, she thought they'd lost their power to wound her. But now that they were here, every day, trying to pretend they were the kind of parents she'd always wanted, she realized the scars were there, and the scabs were rubbing raw.

Her mother startled Lee as she entered the kitchen. "Lee?"

Lee turned around. "I'm sorry, Mom. Guess I haven't been the best conversationalist tonight."

"Your dad didn't mean anything by bringing up the store."

"I know. I'm just touchy, I guess."

"We both know where it came from."

Lee wasn't sure what to say to that. She couldn't deny that her relationship with her parents was rocky at best. But she didn't want to hurt her mother by saying so, so she said nothing.

After a long pause, her mother said, "Your grandmother used to tell me there was a special connection between a mother and a daughter. She'd tell me that I was throwing it away, that you needed me. But you always seemed so self-reliant. You lived in your own world, and you seemed fine with the way things were."

"I wasn't really self-reliant. It was an act I put on out of necessity."

"I was busy at the firm. I loved what I did. But that didn't mean I didn't love you. I argued with my mother. Told her that you and I had a fine relationship, but we didn't, did we?"

Lee thought about lying. Telling her mother they were okay, that they had a fine relationship would be an easy out, but she couldn't say the words.

"We still don't," her mother said quietly. "Part of why we're here is because I'd like to change that, if it's not too late."

"You're not sick, are you? Some dire disease that has you reconsidering your life?"

Her mom laughed. "Nothing like that. I've just had time for reflection and realized what I lost out on."

"Mom, we're just different. We want and expect different things. We're not the type of mother and daughter who are likely to spend a day at the spa, or even shopping. My idea of a good time is a walk on the beach, yours is a column of figures. I think being a success is being happy, you think it's measured in your bank account. It's not that you're a bad mother, or I'm a bad daughter, we're just different. But I need you to know, I love you."

"I love you, too. And my mother was right. There is a connection. We're here because I felt that you needed me. I may not be a great mother, but I know you're not happy. This last year, you've found your peace and achieved a measure of contentment, but you're not happy. You're just going through the motions. You've found a safe rhythm to your life and you're clinging to it. At first I thought I'd come here and push you to focus on the store. But you're right, that would be my solution. It's not yours. The store is a means to an end, a way to support yourself and showcase what you do. Growing it into something bigger won't make you happy. And no matter what you think of my parenting skills, I want you to be happy."

Lee couldn't remember her mother ever talking to her like this. Not ever. She felt her eyes fill with tears and blinked hard.

"Thanks." Her voice sounded husky. "That means a lot. And maybe you're right, maybe I'm not bursting-at-the-seams happy, but after last year, finding a measure of contentment is enough."

"No. It's not enough…not for you. And I'm not leaving until I'm convinced you've found your way back to who you used to be. I think Adam's part of what you're looking for."

"Adam and I might be having a nice little visit, but it can't be anything more. He's leaving soon. And even if he wasn't, whatever we have couldn't go much further."

"Why? We can see the sparks."

"Sparks aren't enough. Adam's invested in his business. And I can't watch someone put work ahead of me again. Adam can't manage a dinner without work interrupting. It's a sure thing he's not for me. After Alan, I swore that I'd rather live alone the rest of my life than play second fiddle to someone's job. "

"It's not just Alan," her mother said softly. "That's what your father and I did as well—put business ahead of you. Like I said, you seemed all right. You had my mother with you, and you two had a connection I couldn't understand. Her stories of the old country, of magic and mystery, they annoyed me, but you, you lived and breathed them. You two lived in this separate world I didn't feel a part of, and still don't. But since we've retired, I've started looking back and I know now that I should have found a way into that world you lived in. I love you, Lee. It's that simple."

Her mother had said those words before, but for the first time she could remember, Lee truly felt them.

She hugged her mother.

They still had baggage, both looked at the world from totally different points of view, but for the first time ever, Lee felt as if they had a bridge, a path to crossing those differences and finding some common ground.

"Now, about you and Adam…" her mother started as they separated.

"Nothing, Mom. We're just friends. Any sparks you sense are just a summer fling that will burn out when Adam leaves."

"We'll see," her mother said, as cryptic as a seer.

"Mom, get that look out of your eye." Lee wasn't sure just what her mom was thinking, and to be honest, she wasn't sure she wanted to know.

"I think I've discovered that maybe I have more of my mother in me than I thought." Her mom hugged her. "Maybe I have a bit of the Irish sight she was always talking about, because I feel there's something more between you and Adam than you want to admit."

"Mom, I've already explained."

"Yes, dear, you have. Maybe you've explained more than you think." Changing the subject, she said, "Now, where's this dessert?"

Chapter Seven

Lee sold one necklace, a bracelet and a small drift-wood sculpture by four the following Monday after-noon. She sat at the small work counter in the corner of the shop, sorting through stones, striving for her usual feeling of all's right in the world.

Her last customer had bought one of Lee's favorite blue-and-green bracelets. She was a new repeat cus-tomer who had discovered Singer's Treasures a few months ago. Since then, she'd stopped in frequently for gifts for friends, and for herself. She was the type of customer who kept Singer's Treasures going.

Lee kept sorting. She was looking for bits of glass whose color and sizes matched, or complemented each other. This was part of the art of crafting jewelry—the part she loved. The bins of glass were like jigsaw pieces. She combed through them until she found just the right grouping. When she finally put enough pieces together and could see the finished product in her mind's eye, it was a *eureka* moment that always left her feeling euphoric.

She was hoping for a spurt of that euphoria because, at the moment, her predominant emotion was confusion. Wondering what to do about her mother's sudden interest in her. She wanted to trust it, to revel in it, but this change of roles made her feel uneasy.

The quiet life she'd so carefully crafted over the last year was in a state of flux. It left her feeling unsettled. She kept hoping the glass sorting would help. It normally did. But today it hadn't so far.

The door opened and Adam walked in without a baby stroller, or baby, for that matter.

They'd spent most of the weekend together with Jessie. They'd gone out to the peninsula and seen the new tourist center, like her mother had suggested. They'd even gone with her mom and dad to play miniature golf on Sunday night. Jessie had been enamored with the plastic putter. She'd hit everything but the golf ball, and Lee hadn't analyzed or worried, she'd just enjoyed.

Enjoyed a night out with her parents and Adam, her childhood nemesis. Who'd have ever thought?

Not her.

But as Adam approached without the baby, she felt a spurt of concern. "Where's Jessie?"

His smile put her at ease…at least, at ease over the baby's safety. "No *hi Adam?* No *nice to see you, Adam?* No—"

She couldn't help but allow a grin herself. "Okay. Hi, Adam. It's so nice to see you. Now, where's Jessie?"

"Your mom and dad borrowed her."

"What?" Her earlier confusion over her parents reasserted itself. What on earth was up with her business-is-life mother and father? Offering to babysit? It was just too…

She couldn't come up with a good description of what it was, but it was unsettling.

"Your mom asked if they could watch her, then suggested since I was free, I come get you and take you out. Just the two us. Alone. An adult thing."

"An adult thing?" Lee asked. "That's what they call it these days? I'm so out of touch with the adult-thing scene."

"A date," he corrected. "Your mom said I should take you out on a real, baby-less date. I just didn't want to spook you by using the word."

"And you're claiming my mom—the woman living in the RV behind my cottage—suggested this?"

Her mom had said she'd sensed the sparks

between Adam and Lee. And Lee was betting this was her attempt to fan them.

Adam nodded. "And right after she was done, your father warned me if I hurt you, he'd hurt me."

"He what?" Lee had thought her mom's change of character was odd, but her father threatening men she dated? That was beyond odd and just plain weird. "I had friends whose fathers would make sure boys they dated knew what was what. One had a father who was a cop. He really laid it on the line. But my dad never even realized I had a date, much less worried about it. My mom either, for that matter. When I announced I was engaged, they asked to who. I'd been dating Alan for two years."

"Well, that's what happened. I had free babysitting on offer, and a death threat all in the space of a few minutes."

"Call Mulder and Scully. This is the weirdest X-File ever. Some pod people are inhabiting my parents' bodies. And you left Jessie with them. They'll probably make her an alien, too."

"From what you told me, I knew it was an odd offer."

"More than odd. Something the Lone Gunmen would put in their paper."

"Two *X-Files* references in a row. Dare I guess what you've been watching lately?"

"I've been buying the seasons on DVD. Although, I freaked myself out a couple times. It's a show meant to be watched in groups, not alone in a cottage on a deserted stretch of lakefront."

"Just call me next time," he offered. "I'd watch with you."

"First an offer of a date, then an offer to watch scary shows? Must be my lucky day."

"Except that whole your-parents-are-pod-people thing."

"Yeah, there's that. It's just weird. They seem to be trying to be…well, parents."

"I thought that's what you wanted?"

She shrugged. "I don't know how I feel about it. Maybe it's too late to be that kind of family."

"What kind of family is that?"

"The kind where the mother offers to babysit and the father threatens guys on your behalf. Maybe when I was younger, but now?" She didn't say, but silently she added, the kind of parents who showed concern.

She knew her parents loved her, but she'd never felt as if she were more than a small blip on their radar screens.

"It's never too late to accept love." His voice softened. "My uncle taught me that."

She reached out and placed her hand lightly on top of his. For a moment, they stayed like that, not talking, nor moving. Just connected, and not just through their hands. Connected on a real person-to-person level. Lee hadn't felt that since her grandmother had passed.

Finally, Adam said, "So, with all this talk of parents, pod people and *X-Files*, the answer to my request to go out was somehow forgotten or lost."

"It was neither forgotten nor lost, just put aside for a minute." She realized she still hadn't answered. "Yes, I'd love to go out."

"Great. How long until you close?"

"Another half hour or so?" she asked. She realized if he wanted, she'd close early. She was half tempted to regardless.

"Great. That's perfect. I'll be back in thirty minutes then." He turned and headed for the door.

"Where are you going?" she called out after him.

"Don't you worry about it."

Lee had said yes.

Adam hadn't realized he'd been nervous until he'd felt the flood of relief when she'd agreed to spend the evening with him.

There were a multitude of reasons he shouldn't be dating Lee. He'd recited the list to himself so many times that he had it memorized.

He was leaving at the end of the month.

His life was already in upheaval with Jessie's care.

He had an every-waking-hour job waiting for him when he got back to New York.

Those were just his reasons for avoiding a relationship. Lee had baggage of her own. The fact was she'd suffered a traumatic end to her marriage, and he wasn't sure she'd totally recovered from that. And she obviously had unresolved issues with her parents.

Yes, it would probably be best for both of them to ignore their growing sense of attraction. It would be safe. Smart.

But Adam had long since learned that you didn't get anywhere by playing it safe.

Starting Delmark, Inc. hadn't been safe. He'd put everything he had and some of Paul's savings on the line when he'd started the small company from nothing. And it had payed off. He'd worked hard to see to it that it did.

But he wasn't sure any amount of work would make whatever this was between Lee and himself end well.

He pushed all his concerns aside and hurried across the park to Snips and Snaps. He wasn't quite sure why he was drawn there. But after meeting Pearly Gates, he knew that she'd at least be able to help figure out where to take Lee…and maybe a few other things as well.

She was at the first hair station talking to a silver-haired man. "Why, I must be livin' right if the powers that be send me two handsome men in one day." She smiled. "So, what brings you in, Adam?"

"I came for advice. But I see that you're busy."

"Don't go gettin' all formal. This is my beau, Buster."

The man extended his hand. "Bartholemew McClinnon."

"Ambassador Bartholemew McClinnon if you want to be all proper," Pearly said. "But don't be. It gives him a swollen head and makes my hair cuttin' that much harder. You can call him just plain ol' Buster, like the rest of us. Keeps him humble."

The ambassador laughed. Adam didn't have to be overly insightful to see that the man was head over heels in love with Pearly Gates.

"Ex-ambassador," he said. "Pearly just likes to show off."

"Hey, it's not every day I get to say I'm dating an ambassador, ex or otherwise."

"Engaged to an ambassador," he corrected.

The gray-haired woman actually blushed as she dangled her ring at Adam.

He gave a long whistle of appreciation. "Well, whatever you call yourself these days, sir, I'd say you have great taste in engagement rings and fiancées. Congratulations." He thrust out his hand. "Adam Benton."

"I remember," the ambassador assured him as they shook.

"Now, what advice did you need?" Pearly asked.

"The name of a restaurant."

"Well, there's the Five and Dine where we all ate the other day."

"No," Adam said. "I mean, the food was great, but

I need something a bit fancier." He paused, then added, "I'm taking Lee out on a date."

"A date, just the two of you? No baby?" Pearly asked.

"Yes."

She smiled. "That does need something fancier. How 'bout Abayte. It's new, down on the bay front. Quiet, romantic and swanky as all get out. Plus the food's great. It's not all so fancy that you're afraid to order."

"We went last night," the ambassador said. "It's a place for memories."

"That's where you proposed?" Adam guessed. They both nodded their heads and cast another one of those hearts flying-between-them sort of looks.

"Abayte sounds like just what I'm looking for. I'll call and get a reservation."

"If they're full, or put you off, mention my name. The ambassador one, not the Buster one." The older gentleman laughed.

"Thanks," he said. "I'd better get going. Lee's closing up the shop soon."

"Adam," Pearly said, "I know it's none of my business—"

"Uh-oh," the ambassador said, warning in his voice. "It never bodes well for a man when Pearly starts a sentence with *I know it's none of my business*."

She shot the ambassador a look and he wisely got quiet. Very quiet.

"As I was sayin'," she started again, "it's none of my business, but I want you to promise you'll be careful of Lee."

"You're the second person to warn me today. Why does everyone think I'd hurt her?" It wasn't that he didn't question the wisdom of getting entangled with Lee Singer. He did. But hurt her? That was the last thing he'd ever do.

"Are you going back to New York at the end of the month?" Pearly asked.

"Yes. My company's there." Normally he'd be chomping at the bit to get back to it. But the last few days he'd realized how very little enthusiasm he had for returning to New York. It wasn't that he wasn't still pulled by his business, but he'd begun to suspect there was something in Erie that pulled at him as well.

"And so you're going to wine and dine Lee, then just leave?" Pearly asked softly.

"I don't know what's going to happen. What I do know is that Lee means something to me, and that something is growing. I want to see just where it leads."

"Just don't hurt her," she warned again. "Now, go get ready for your date."

Adam hurried out. First Lee's father, now Pearly Gates. He wasn't planning on hurting Lee. But he suddenly wondered if his growing attraction to her would end up hurting him.

* * *

Adam had brought Lee flowers.

Pink roses. Had they been red, she might have felt uncomfortable.

Lee didn't think whatever they had between them was at a red-rose level. But the small pink tea roses weren't as intimidating. She nervously fingered one of the roses' petals as she drank in the atmosphere of Abayte.

She remembered how excited Perry Square neighbor Sarah Donovan had been when she'd gotten the contract to decorate the new upscale restaurant.

Lee would have to make sure and let her know that she'd done a wonderful job. The dining room had a very classy, nautical feel to it. Soothing shades of blue and gray were the predominant colors, and soft lighting, accented by candles on every table, completed the perfect atmosphere.

"Everything all right?" Adam asked.

"It's wonderful," she assured him. "I was just drinking in the room. It's beautiful."

"Not as beautiful as y—" he started.

Lee cut him off with a snort. "Don't you dare feed me a line like that, Matty Benton. Remember me? I'm the girl you chased with a snake, saying it was my long-lost cousin. Snake girls by their very definition aren't beautiful, and this particular snake girl doesn't respond well to canned lines."

"You seemed quiet and it made me nervous because that used to signal you were thinking." He didn't look nervous. He looked as if he was enjoying this.

"Why would my thinking make you nervous?"

"If you recall the snake incident, you must also recall your revenge."

"Telling Angie Thomas you liked her wasn't a bad revenge."

"It was because I did like her, and being a senior, she wasn't much interested in a twelve-year-old boy. If I recall correctly she told me that my crush was *cute*. I avoided her for a long time after that. I mean, *cute?*"

Lee smiled. "Well, she was right. You were cute. Now, see that wasn't nearly as pat as your whole more-beautiful comment."

As they ate, Lee said, "Tell me about your company. I've noticed how busy you've been, despite the fact you're supposed to be on sabbatical."

"This turned out to be absolutely the worst time for me to leave. We're on the cusp of a major expansion into a brand-new market. Rather than just working on computer systems, we've actually developed and patented a new chip. Rather than sell the rights, we're going to attempt manufacturing it ourselves. Starting our own research department and…"

Lee was totally caught up in Adam's excitement at seeing his dreams unfold.

"I'm so happy for your success," she said. And though his nonstop work schedule would drive her crazy in short order, she could see he thrived on the challenge. "Can I ask just how Jessie's going to fit into your life, since work is obviously going to be busier, at least until your expansion's complete?"

"That's why I'm here. Trying to decide if I can give her what she needs and still cope with the company's needs. This is the biggest lull I'll have for a few months, so I'm taking the time to work things out. My right-hand man, Darius, is ready to assume more responsibility, but still, this next year is going to be brutal. I don't know if I can do it all. I know a lot of working moms do, but…"

"The fact you're worried about it, that you're taking the time to really think it through shows how much you care about Jessie. I'm sure you'll take care of her best interests."

Maybe that's what her parents had tried to do. Realizing they had a growing business, and a growing child, they'd seen to it that she'd had her grandmother when they hadn't been with her. Maybe, like Adam, they'd simply tried to do the best they could for her and for themselves.

Did their visit mean that maybe, like Adam, they doubted their attempt at getting the balance right?

"You're quiet again," Adam said. "I hope I'm not the target of this new bout of thinking. Care to share?"

"What you said about Jessie, about working things out in her best interest. It got me thinking about my parents, and their new attempt to become more hands-on in my life."

"Is it all so bad?" he asked.

"It's…" She searched for the right word and finally settled on, "Weird."

"But I thought that's what you always wanted."

He was right. Having her parents take a more active role in her life was what she'd wanted…when she was younger. Now, she was older and wasn't sure how to deal with their attention.

The waitress came and cleared away their dinner dishes. "Would you like dessert?" she asked.

Before Lee could say no, Adam ordered a sinful-sounding chocolate tart and coffee.

Lee grinned. "I'll have the same."

After the waitress left, Lee said, "You forced me into it. I mean, I couldn't let you eat all alone."

Adam laughed.

She searched for some new topic, but before she could come up with something else, Adam spoke, "What you said about your parents. It's not just concern or being part of your life, it's love. When I went to live with my uncle, I was a real jerk. I made his life miserable. I blamed him for not finding me sooner, and I blamed him for finding me when he did and taking me away from someplace that was starting to feel like home."

"I'm sorry."

"Don't be. Paul was the best thing that ever happened to me. It took time for us to develop a relationship. To get to know each other. Give your parents some time—see what happens."

"About us," she started, not sure what to say.

"Let's table that discussion and anything else remotely serious. I've wined and dined you, brought you flowers. I think the next step to a perfect first official date is to gorge ourselves on the chocolate tarts, then take a walk along the bay. What do you think?"

Lee felt a wave of relief. "Sounds wonderful to me. You're on."

After finishing their desserts, which were beyond decadent in Lee's book, they left the restaurant and walked up State Street to the bay-front highway, then along the sidewalk, drinking in the sights in silence. The quiet was fine with Lee. She didn't want to think, didn't want to analyze. She just wanted to enjoy this moment with this man.

They reached the empty amphitheater, and climbed the grassy hill to its crest just as the sun began to slip behind the peninsula. A few children ran about on the playground below, out of their line of sight. Their occasional squeals were the only sounds intruding on the twilight.

"Lee." Adam turned her toward him, and she could see the question in his eyes and gave her answer by kissing him with a hunger she'd forgotten existed.

Want. She wanted this man, wanted to feel his body pressed to hers, wanted his arms wrapped around her. The want was changing into something more akin to need.

They parted, both a little breathless from the kiss.

"Wow," was Adam's eloquent comment.

It made Lee laugh. "Wow, yourself."

"Since there are kids just below us on the playground, it occurs to me that we're tempting fate. I think it's best if we head back to the car before they find us."

"You're right."

He took her hand and held it as they started to retrace their steps.

Walking next to Adam, Lee realized for the first time this year she felt truly alive. She felt connected to the world. She had Adam to thank for that.

She drew in a deep breath.

Alive.

Chapter Eight

The next week passed in a warm summer haze. Her mother and father's RV was still parked behind her cottage. Lee's old resentments were fading. And she spent as much time with Adam and Jessie as possible.

She felt buoyant and light.

She couldn't remember the last time she'd felt so…well, just plain good. She still had no idea where her relationship with Adam was going, but she was appreciating the ride and trying not to let worries about the future intrude.

She felt lost when they were apart, and practically bubbly when they were together.

Friday evening as she watched Jessie splash a wave on the shore, Lee realized that the almost constant ache she'd lived with the last year had faded.

It wasn't that she'd forgotten her baby, just that when she remembered now there was no sharp pain that left her breathless, just a soft feeling of regret for what might have been. She felt as if she could finally say goodbye to that painful chapter. Not forget, just move on. Move toward something new.

She crawled into bed that night, looking forward to the next morning. They were going to take Jessie to the park again.

Lee felt as if she'd just closed her eyes when something woke her up. She sat upright and for a befuddled moment tried to figure out what was wrong.

She realized the sound that had woken her was her phone.

"Hello?" Her voice was thick with sleep. She glanced at the clock. Four thirty-three. There was no such thing as a good call at four thirty-three in the morning. "Hello?"

"Lee, it's me, Adam. Could you come over. I think Jessie's sick."

Lee's heart was racing as she ran the short distance that spanned the cottages. She didn't even bother to knock, just threw open the door and hurried into the living room.

Adam was sitting in the rocking chair, holding

Jessie. The toddler's head was resting on his shoulder. "Thanks. I didn't know what else to do. She's got a fever. I gave her some acetaminophen, but she's still so warm."

Lee had an I-don't-know-nothin'-about-birthin'-no-babies panic moment, then a feeling of assurance. "When I was a kid my grandmother used to give me a tepid bath when I had a fever. I don't know if it helped, but it always felt heavenly. Want to try that?"

"Sure. I'll try anything at this point. She's just so miserable." Jessie wasn't the only one who looked miserable. Adam's face was pinched with anxiety.

Lee wished she could make him feel better, but knew that nothing would until Jessie was right, so she hurried into the small bathroom and started the water in the claw-foot cast-iron tub. A moment later, Adam brought Jessie in. She was flushed looking and her eyes were glassy.

"Hey, baby," Lee crooned. "I hear you're not feeling all that good." She began taking Jessie's pj's off. "To be honest, Adam doesn't look any better, does he?"

"I don't think I've done more than doze all night. If I look half as bad as I feel right now, I must be scary."

"Not quite scary." No, as a matter of fact, seeing him so worked up over Jessie was endearing. "But bad enough. Why don't you go lie down for a few minutes and I'll give Jessie here a bath, then get her in fresh pj's."

"I can help."

"I know, but humor me."

"Well, maybe for a few minutes." He started out of the bathroom, then turned around. "Thanks. Other than my uncle and Cathie, there's never been anyone I could call in the middle of the night and just say *come,* and know that they'd be here. That's something for me to realize, Lee. You can't know just how much it means."

Before she could respond, he turned and hurried out of the room.

Lee brushed at a drop of suspicious moisture on her cheek. "Must have been splashed starting your bath," she said to Jessie, although even the sick toddler didn't seem to buy the explanation.

"Your cousin is very special, isn't he?"

Instead of her normal, happy chatter, Jessie made a sad moan in response.

"Come on, sweetie. Let's have a nice bath."

Lee forced herself to concentrate on the baby. Fifteen minutes later, she had Jessie dried, powdered and in a fresh pair of pajamas.

Lee carried her out to the living room and sat in the rocker with her. Adam was sprawled across the couch, dead to the world.

Lee began to rock back and forth, and soon Jessie's body became deadweight in her arms. Still, she rocked, humming one of her grandmother's favorite lullabies in the toddler's ear.

She stole another look at Adam. Tonight, his concern for Jessie was so evident, she'd had a sneaky feeling that here was a man she could love. Moments when he laughed with her, when he held her, she could believe that they had a chance at something. But then he'd sink back into a hyper work-is-every-thing zone, and she'd worry that falling for Adam Benton would be another big mistake.

And this time she wasn't sure any amount of time would allow her to recover.

Adam woke up feeling groggy as he tried to decide where he was and when it was.

Slowly he pried open his sleep-heavy lids and his eyes came into focus on Lee. She had fallen asleep in the rocker, cradling Jessie.

He thought about sitting up, but didn't want to disturb her. Instead, he simply watched them both.

He'd come to Erie to make a decision for Jessie's future…for his future. He knew if he kept his cousin, he'd have to find a way to balance what was right for the company and the same for Jessie.

Since college, Delmark had been his sole focus. He had dated, but never anyone for too long, never too seriously. Letting someone in, even if she was so young—especially if she was so young—would mean concessions at work.

Concessions he wasn't sure he wanted to make. Delmark was on the cusp of something big. He'd brought the company that far. A diversification that would make them stronger.

He'd done that.

And until lately, he'd thought the company would be his life's work.

But sitting here in the wee hours of the morning, watching Lee and Jessie, he knew that if his company was all he had to show for his life, it would be a shallow sort of prize.

And with stark clarity, he suddenly knew he wanted more.

He'd like to think all his doubts about keeping and raising Jessie evaporated, but they didn't. He knew despite them though, he was going to keep her. Which meant he had to rethink his role at Delmark. He wouldn't let go of the reins, but maybe ease up on them a bit. Life needed balance.

I work to live, not live to work. That's what Lee had told him.

For too many years he'd lived to work and had forgotten to live a life. For Jessie's sake, he was going to have to change that. He recognized that fact, thanks to Lee.

Lee.

What was he going to do about Lee?

If she lived in New York, or he lived in Erie, there would be no question. He'd continue seeing her and let their relationship develop. But they lived seven hours apart. How was he going to reconcile that?

Adam wasn't sure how long he stayed on the couch, watching the women in his life and making tentative plans, but as the sky grew brighter, he had at least an idea of what he wanted, what he hoped for.

As Lee began to stir, Adam got off the couch and walked across the room.

"Here, let me get her from you," he whispered as he deftly scooped up Jessie from Lee's arms. Their hands grazed each other and he felt a stir of awareness.

He knew they both looked a bit worse for wear after their long night with Jessie, but as their eyes met, he also knew he'd never seen anyone look more beautiful.

"Morning," he said, his voice still soft. He took Jessie but didn't move from the spot. He wanted to reach out and touch Lee, but since his arms were full of sleeping toddler, he simply settled for standing near her. "I can't thank you enough for the help last night. Although, I didn't mean to crash and leave you carrying the brunt of it."

Lee stretched, reaching for the sky and tipping left and right to work out the kinks. Adam's earlier awareness moved to desire in that split second.

"Adam. You all right?" she asked.

He swallowed hard. "Sure. Fine. Just tired."

"She's much cooler now. Since she's on the mend and still sleeping, I should probably head home and let you get a bit more sleep if you can."

"I know that she's probably not going to be up for the park, but can we still get together?"

Lee smiled. "Sure. I'd like that."

"Great. I've been doing some thinking. We should talk later."

"Just come over whenever the two of you are up and moving." Gently she reached out and brushed Jessie's wild hair off her forehead before placing a light kiss on it.

Adam wished she'd touch him as tenderly, but she didn't. She just gave him a small wave and left.

He carried Jessie into the bedroom.

Okay, so he'd get some more sleep, but then he'd put his plan into motion.

It was almost noon before Adam and Jessie came over to Lee's cottage.

"Come on in," she called through the screen door. "You're just in time. I'm making omelettes."

"Eggs. Mmm," Adam said, setting Jessie down on the floor.

Jessie made an immediate beeline for the tissue box on the end table, then plopped onto the floor and began pulling tissues out, one by one, and shredding them.

Lee laughed at the pile of tissue accumulating in front of Jessie. "I'd say the patient has made a complete recovery."

"And I think I found the culprit. A new tooth."

"That's so cool." Lee knew it was goofy, that all babies got teeth, but she felt as if Jess had come in and handed a report card with straight *A*s. "Pretty soon you'll be thinking about braces."

"God forbid. Cathie had a perfect smile, and I'll just hope Jess does, too."

She realized he'd responded as if he'd be there when Jessie needed braces. Lee wondered if he'd made a decision, but was almost afraid to ask. If he said no, her heart might break. So, she said, "If you open the left-hand cupboard there are Cheerios for Jessie. And I bought a sippy cup for her. It's right next to it. There's milk and apple juice in the fridge. If the tooth is still bothering her, the cold liquid might help."

"You've thought of everything."

"Not quite everything, but every now and again I get a few things right." She took the mushrooms out of the pan and placed them on a waiting plate, then dumped the egg mixture into the hot pan. "I hope mushroom-and-cheese is okay?"

"Great."

"The coffee's hot."

The scene felt homey as Lee added the mushrooms into the omelet and covered the whole thing with a few slices of provolone cheese.

Adam picked up Jessie from her mound of tissues and set her in the booster seat that Lee had also bought. He handed her breakfast, or maybe *brunch* was a better description, and the toddler gamely played with the Cheerios as Adam sipped at his cup.

Lee leaned over the table. "Smile, Jessie."

The small white tip of a tooth was evident.

"She'll look a bit snaggletoothed and definitely

lopsided until the other one comes through to balance it out," Adam said. "But I hope it waits at least a few weeks. I don't think I could do another night like that right away."

Lee turned back to the stove and slid the omelet from the pan, cut it in half and moved part to a second plate, before carrying them to the table.

"Here you go."

"It looks great." Adam took a bite and made an appreciative noise as he ate it. "Tastes better."

"Thanks. Although, omelets are pretty simple to make."

Adam swallowed his second bite. "It's better than I can do. Potato salad. That's my one and only dish. And as much as I like it, it's not quite what I want for breakfast."

They ate in companionable silence for a few minutes as Jessie chatted to the cereal she was busily throwing here and there.

"You said you wanted to talk to me?" Lee asked.

"I have a favor." Adam paused. "A big favor."

"You know I'm here for you," Lee said, with no hesitation.

For the last year, she'd kept to herself and avoided relying on someone, or having someone rely on her. But she realized she could count on Adam and was pleased he felt he could ask her for help as well. "What do you need?"

"Darius called this morning, and I have to go back

to the city for just a couple days. One of our biggest clients is in town and things aren't going well. We can't afford to lose the account and Darius feels like he's in over his head. Could you keep Jessie a few days?"

"So you can go back to work."

"I don't have any day care arranged for her yet, so I thought if you kept her here I could take care of business and even start lining up some things for when I go back."

Lee finally gave voice to the question that had been nagging at her. "So you are keeping her then?"

"Yes." There was happiness, tinged with more than a little nervousness in his smile. "I don't know if I'm doing the right thing, but I can't let her go."

"What about her grandparents, Cathie's parents?"

"I'll need to talk to them as soon as they get back from their trip and make sure that they understand that I'd never cut them out of Jessie's life. And there are other ideas I have that might do for all of us." He took another sip of coffee. "Needless to say, I have a lot to do."

"Yes, I see that. And yes, I'll keep her." She forced herself to smile. Adam was keeping Jessie. That was good news. They'd be leaving soon—she made sure her smile didn't slip at the thought. She didn't want Adam to know how much she'd miss them both.

"You're sure?" he asked. "I thought I'd leave on Monday. It will only be for a couple days."

"Right. No problem."

"What about work?"

"I'll see if Juliet will take over more hours in the shop, and whatever she can't cover, I'll either take Jessie with me or see if Mom will watch her. Don't worry. I'll handle it."

"I'm sure you will."

He leaned over the table and kissed her, long and hard. "When I come back, we'll talk some more."

Chapter Nine

Adam stared out his office window, between the two skyscrapers across the street. He could barely make out the sun.

Normally he didn't think about the weather when he was at work. He'd made Delmark a success with his ability to use tunnel vision to focus on the business and its clients. But nothing had felt the same since he'd walked into the building yesterday. An office that had seemed like home for so many years suddenly felt oppressive.

"…and finally, we have to…" Darius droned on, and as hard as Adam tried to follow the thread of what his friend was saying, he found it difficult.

His thoughts were back in Erie, with Lee and Jessie.

He wondered if it was a sunny day there, if they were out for a walk on the beach, or if they were sitting on the cottage porch.

Maybe Jessie was shredding paper, or…

He'd spoken to Lee before coming into the office this morning. She'd assured him that everything was fine. Jessie was thriving, her parents were helping and playing doting grandparents. "I think you should bring an extra suitcase with you. You're going to need it to get all Jessie's things back home. And you may need to purchase a separate carryall for the huge stuffed dolphin they bought her."

She'd talked of Jessie's activities, talked of her parents, but had said very little about herself. She hadn't mentioned missing him.

He realized how much he wanted her to. It would put them on a semi-equal footing, because he was missing her like crazy.

"Earth calling Adam. Have you heard a word I've said?" Darius chuckled. "Oh, how far the mighty have fallen. Tell me about her."

Adam had met Darius when he'd been invited into a local high school's business class to speak. Darius had stayed after the class to talk. Adam had been impressed and had offered the boy a part-time job. He'd encouraged Darius to go to college and let him juggle his work schedule around his classes. Adam had been sitting next to Darius's family at his college graduation.

At first, theirs had been a mentor-mentoree sort of relationship, but when Darius had come to work full-time at Delmark, it had gradually shifted. Darius wasn't just an employee. Not just some boy Adam had mentored. He was a friend.

A friend who appeared to be enjoying a laugh at Adam's expense.

"You know you want to tell me about her," Darius teased, his dark eyes alight.

For a moment, Adam was reminded of the young joker he'd taken under his wing. "Her? Well, she's a year and a half old, and has this wispy blond hair that makes me think of Einstein. She's—"

"Funny, Adam. Not Jessie, though I imagine you're thinking about her, too. The other *her.*"

"I don't know what other *her* you're talking about. I'm just distracted, thinking about Jessie and who should raise her. Wondering if I've made the right decision for her."

"Ha. You're keeping her. I never doubted it. You like to pretend you're a loner, but we both know that's not the truth. You'll call Jessie's grandparents before you go back to Erie and invite them to have an active role in her life, but you're keeping her. At first I'd have said you'd do it because you loved Paul and Cathie, but it's not just that. You've fallen in love with Jessie. And the baby isn't who's on your mind right now."

"So, you've been taking mind-reading classes since I left?" Adam tried to give Darius a stern, threatening sort of look, but his friend's smile said he wasn't buying it. "Well, if I'm not worrying about what to do with Jessie, what am I thinking about?"

"Lee." Darius smiled. "She's the one for you. And for the first time ever, you're torn. You love Delmark, but you love her, too. She's in Erie, Delmark's here. You're not sure how you're going to work that out. Figuring out what to do with Jessie was much easier."

Adam shook his head. "Don't look so smug. Someday you're going to fall, and when you do I'll be the one laughing."

"Nope. I've seen too many friends go through this. I'm just going to concentrate on business. You see, my boss just gave me a lot more responsibility, and I suspect there will be even more heading my way soon."

"Keep it up, Darius. You're just tempting fate. I thought I had my life all mapped out, and suddenly, here I am, a baby and a woman occupying my every waking thought. Your time's coming."

"Not very likely, old man. I'm only twenty-five. I have a lot of years left to play the field. But back to the question at hand, what are you going to do?"

That certainly was the question. Adam had been toying with it since he'd left Erie.

What was he going to do?

* * *

Lee and Jessie fell into a routine. They'd start their day with a quick breakfast, then a walk along the beach. Lee invested in a baby backpack, which made carrying the squirming toddler easier. They'd take their walk, then Lee would let her get down to play. Lee would work through Jessie's nap.

Juliet had been thrilled to take on the extra hours. So happy in fact, Lee wondered if she should consider making it permanent. Juliet loved working in the store. For Lee, it was a chore. She'd have to work up the numbers and see if she could afford more time off.

But for right now, she just concentrated on having a wonderful time with the baby.

Okay, since she was mobile, maybe Lee should use the term *toddler*. Because Jessie wasn't just mobile, she was fast.

She had single-handedly unwound every toilet-paper roll, and shredded every tissue and napkin in the cottage, then she'd found a ream of computer printer paper and had gone to town. Lee tried to be strict, but truly, Jessie had so much fun, she barely managed a good scold.

The highlight of each of the last three days was talking to Adam. He'd call in the morning, and again in the evening to ask about every detail of Jessie's day. Of Lee's day. And Lee would ask about his.

Pearly had been right—his work was his passion

every bit as much as her art was. But even knowing that, she couldn't quite shake her old resentments, though she tried to put them aside.

"Do you miss me?" he asked unexpectedly on Tuesday night.

"Do you want me to?" she countered, taken aback by the bluntness of his question and not quite sure how he wanted her to answer—how she wanted to answer.

He paused a moment. "Yes, I believe I do, mainly because I miss you." The admission was soft and unexpected.

"I miss you, too."

"You don't sound happy about it. Listen, I'm not sure what exactly you want to call what we have between us—"

"Truth is, I'd rather not give it a name just yet, if that's okay." Lee was afraid to give it a name. Names had power and the feelings she had for Adam were powerful enough on their own.

"This thing that shall remain nameless is hitting me fast and it's strong," Adam admitted.

"For now, let's just talk about Jessie."

Adam allowed the conversation to shift, much to Lee's relief. "So, are you getting any work done? I know how… um, active, Jess can be."

Lee laughed. "That's a very kind word. And yes, I am getting more work done than I imagined I could. I've just gotten creative at finding the time. I work when she naps, and after she's in bed. I'm finding that because I know I'm on a limited schedule, I work a bit harder."

"Good."

"To be honest, it's a relief."

"Relief?"

"I've worried that if I ever have a baby, I'd put my work first, like my parents did. But Jessie's first, work's second. I'll confess, cleaning's coming dead last. Thankfully, having a small cottage means there's not much that needs to be done."

"I'll be home tomorrow and can help, if you want."

"So soon?" she asked.

"Hey, don't sound so excited."

"It's just…" She paused then slowly added, "When you're back, we'll have to talk about us. And truth be told, I'll miss Jessie. A lot. I've enjoyed having her to myself."

"I'll share her. How about when I get back tomorrow night the three of us spend time together?"

"That would be nice."

"Then we'll talk about what's happening between us."

To be honest, that didn't sound so nice. Whenever someone talked about talking in that particular tone, it simply didn't bode well.

Adam couldn't believe how nervous he was. He'd left earlier than he'd planned simply because he couldn't wait to get home to Jessie and Lee.

Lee obviously had heard his SUV because as he pulled up at the cottages, she was immediately outside with Jessie. She set the toddler on the ground and Jess did a toddly version of a run to Adam, crying, "Da, da, da, da," the whole time.

His heart melted as he brought her to him and hugged her tight. He couldn't believe how much he'd missed her. He realized she'd become a part of his life, and he knew his decision about her upbringing was the right one.

Just as he knew when he looked up and found Lee smiling one of her dazzling smiles at him that some choices weren't ours to make. They were simply presented to us as a done deal.

Lee was a done deal, as far as his emotions were concerned.

"Welcome home," she said.

"It's good to be back. I missed you both." He paused and added, "A lot."

"We missed you as well. So, how was the trip?"

"Seven hours is a long drive."

"We didn't expect you until much later."

"I know. I didn't plan to leave so early, but I…" He was going to tell her. He was going to say the words and put his feelings out on the table.

He wasn't sure what her reaction would be.

He knew what he hoped it would be, but the thing about Lee was she kept him guessing.

"You?" she prompted.

"I—"

"Yoo-hoo," Mrs. Singer hollered as she rounded Lee's cottage corner and came into view, Mr. Singer on her heels. "I saw the vehicle and wanted to come over and welcome you home. Lee and Jessie missed you."

"That's good because I missed them."

"And I know that Lee's been chasing after Jessie all day and trying to get her work, so was thinking that I'd make dinner tonight."

Mrs. Singer looked so pleased that Adam forced himself to swallow his disappointment. "That is kind of you," he said.

"But we were going to do something together. Just the three of us," Lee finished.

Lee's mother's happy expression disappeared. "Oh, well, of course you would. I don't know what I was thinking. You go and have a good time."

She smiled at them both, but Adam could see that Mrs. Singer was trying to put on a brave face.

"I'm sorry, Mom. I mean—"

"What Lee means is," Adam broke in, "there's not a place in Erie we'd rather be, so get cooking."

Mrs. Singer grinned. "Only if you're sure."

"I'm sure."

"Lee?" her mother asked.

Lee smiled and nodded. "Yes, I'm sure, Mom. That is kind of you."

"Not kind. Just motherly. We'll get everything ready. Show up at six."

"Yes, ma'am." Adam's phone rang. He checked the caller ID. "I have to take this," he said apologetically.

"Sure," Lee said as she turned back to her mother and discussions about tonight's dinner.

Adam had seen a flicker of something in her expression. Disappointment? Annoyance? He wasn't sure and didn't have time to ask. He flipped the phone open. "Yes?"

"I've set up those talks," Darius started.

His friend continued on about the meeting, but Adam's thoughts kept drifting to Lee.

It didn't take a rocket scientist to see that she hated it when he got business calls. And as much as he might try to minimize them, the nature of what he did meant there would always be business calls.

Could he really reconcile her wants and the business's needs?

Lee could hardly keep her eyes off Adam. Jessie had dozed off while he was holding her. Lee had offered to go lay her down, but Adam had shaken his head. "She's so busy that this is about the only time she's still enough to hold."

Watching him talk with her parents while holding Jessie melted her heart. He'd changed during his time in Erie. She'd noticed his cell phone hadn't rung once during dinner and he seemed more relaxed than when he'd arrived.

"Hey," he said.

"Sorry. I was drifting."

"Lee's always been a daydreamer." Her mother was busy gathering plates.

"I think it's one of her more charming traits," Adam assured her.

Lee shot him a smile of gratitude.

Her mother replied. "It just so happens that I do as well. Dessert everyone?"

"Let me help you, Mom." Lee took some of the empty dishes and followed her mother into the motor home's small kitchenette. "It's in the refrigerator, dear. That peanut-butter-and-chocolate-pudding dish."

"Thank you."

"You're welcome. I know you like it. Despite Adam's kind words, I know I'm not a great cook, but since it doesn't require cooking, I'm generally safe serving it."

"No, I meant thank you for outside. For saying you didn't mind my drifting. And while I'm at it, let me thank you for all the help with Jessie the last couple of days."

"You're welcome. It was our pleasure. She's a delight. As well as a reminder of how much we missed with you."

"Mom, don't."

"I won't. I realize I can't go back, but I appreciate you giving me another chance."

"There was never a question. You're my mother. I love you."

Her mom pulled her into a tight hug. "I love you, too. Now before we get any more emotional, let's get back out there."

Her mother served the dessert and, as they all settled in, Adam spoke, "I have an announcement. I've made my decision about Jessie's future. I talked to her grandparents while I was in New York and she's staying with me. But rather than hiring a nanny, her grandparents are going to watch her on days I work. If she proves to be too much for them to handle, I'll look into finding a sitter a couple days a week. I think it will be the best scenario for Jessie. She'll be surrounded by people who love her."

Lee hugged him. "I'm so happy for both of you."

"I just couldn't let her go. I love her."

"I know."

Lee's parents were offering congratulations.

"This calls for a picture," Lee's mother said excitedly. She started rummaging through her bag.

"Mom, I'm not so much the picture person."

"Your mom's just bought a new digital camera," Lee's father explained. "There's no getting out of it, so you might as well get used to it. I've got pictures of me on pretty much every square inch of the RV."

"Now, first Adam and Jessie." Before Lee's eyes,

her mother turned into a virtual Steven Spielberg, directing her shots. "Now, Lee, let's get all three of you."

"This is Adam and Jessie's celebration. I'm not in it."

"Still, I want group shots of everyone." Her father had been right. There was no getting out of it, so Lee joined Adam and Jessie, posing with the lake as their backdrop.

"Now, Aston, go get Jessie. I want one of just Lee and Adam."

They stood close, but not quite touching. "Come on, you two. Neither of you is contagious. Adam, put your arm around her."

He did and, without meaning to, Lee found herself leaning into the slightly staged connection.

Her mother clicked off several shots.

"Now, Adam, maybe you'd get one of Lee and us?"

"I'd be happy to, Mrs. Singer."

Lee found herself sandwiched between her parents. She didn't think they'd ever taken a family picture before.

As Adam snapped the shot, Jessie, seeing her window of opportunity, made a mad dash for the water.

Lee left the shot and went after the toddler, Adam on their heels after he'd handed the camera to her mother.

Neither of them managed to catch Jessie before she hit the water. She was happily splashing, and

Adam put an arm around Lee's shoulder. "She does love the water," he said as he left Lee's side to retrieve his niece.

"Yoo-hoo, you two," Lee's mom hollered. They turned and her shutter popped open and closed in rapid succession. "Now, that's going to be a keeper."

They went back to the picnic table, and Adam got dry clothes out of the diaper bag and started changing Jessie. "You're a mess," he said, laughing.

"I'm so glad you're keeping her," Lee said.

"Jessie's lucky to have you," her normally quiet father said. "That's what we tried to do for Lee, see to it she was always cared for by someone who loved her as much as we did."

Lee knew that's exactly what her parents had done. When they worked she was with her grandmother. When they didn't, she was with them. It might not have been everything she wished for, but her parents had done their best, just as Adam was trying to do his best for Jessie.

Years of feeling neglected faded and Lee realized how lucky she was to have spent her life surrounded by those who loved her. She got up and hugged her father.

At first he seemed a bit surprised, but then his arms wrapped around her and he hugged her in return.

"I love you, Dad," she whispered in his ear.

"Me, too."

Her mother got up and headed into the RV. "Mom, where are you going?"

"I have a bottle of wine in the kitchen. We're going to toast Adam's new family."

Adam had tucked Jessie in bed before joining Lee on the porch. They sat on the bench, close, and he wondered where to start. Despite the fact that Mrs. Singer had made a delicious meal, his stomach was tied in knots.

"I thought about you a lot while I was away." It was the best opening he could come up with.

"I did, too," Lee said. "I'll miss you when you leave next week."

"I need to talk to you about that. I can't stay the final week. Things are moving faster than Darius and I anticipated. Taking Delmark down a new avenue is going to take more work than I realized—and I realized a lot of work. My taking time off now wasn't best timed, but I knew that things would only get busier until we have the new division set up. I've made my decision about Jessie, and simply can't justify being away from work any longer. And—"

"You don't owe me an explanation," Lee blurted.

He closed the small gap that separated them so that they sat thigh to thigh. "Maybe I don't owe you, but I want to explain."

He took her hand and, feeling less than confident about her response, said, "I need you to know how it is before I ask you to…come with us. Come to New York with Jessie and me. I know there's something growing between us, and I thought we'd have more time to see what it was, but—"

"But you have to get back to work. And with things getting busier there, and adding a baby to your household, just where would I fit in?" Lee asked.

"I don't know. I haven't sorted it all out. All I know is I don't want whatever we have between us to end here."

She took her hand out of his and shook her head. "Adam, I can't."

"You don't have to move in with me. That's not what I meant. Your own place. I talked to Darius and he's found somewhere you could sublet. The rent's about as good as you're going to get in the city, and it's close to me."

"You planned this? Asking me?"

The few days he'd been gone had felt like years. He'd missed Jessie and Lee. It hadn't taken long for him to decide to at least ask her to come with him. If he didn't, he'd spend the rest of his life wondering…regretting.

"I know it's fast—"

"Fast?" she repeated. "It's warp speed. I knew my ex all through college, and look what happened with us. You and I have only known each other a few weeks. What chance would we have?"

"More than a few weeks." He took her hand again. "Lee, we've known each other since we were kids. Back when I was Matty, the bane of your existence. And you were Mary Eileen, a girl who dreamed."

Dreams.

Lee fingered the necklace she still kept in her pocket. She'd been carrying it like some kind of talisman since Adam had moved into her cottage. Her first piece of jewelry, long forgotten among her old mementos, had suddenly become important.

What she was sure of was that this insane idea of Adam's wouldn't work. Couldn't.

"Adam, I'm flattered," she started.

"That sounds as ominous as when a woman says, *You're a nice guy but.*"

"You are a nice guy, but I can't come to New York. My life is here." She'd worked hard to rebuild her life after her marriage had failed. After she'd lost her baby. She'd found a measure of peace. Found a new life. How could she just walk away from that?

How could Adam ask her to?

"You could build a new life with me and Jessie," Adam said. "You could sell your jewelry as easily in New York as in Erie. Hell, Juliet can run the shop here, and you can open another in New York. She can ship you beach glass. I'll help you figure out a way to do whatever it takes. I just want to have a chance."

She felt a wave of anger. He expected her to give up everything to follow him? "Let's turn this around.

You stay here. Let your friend Darius run the company. Give up your job, your home, the life you know, and stay here with me. No more ten-plus-hour workdays. No more phone calls day and night. No more working weekends. You can find something else here in Erie. Something nine to five. You can take over management of Singer's Treasures, if you like. Or maybe start a small computer business here."

"I can't. It's not just me." He dropped her hand and slid to the edge of the bench. "Listen, I built the company from the ground up. Darius can't do it alone. At least, not yet. He's handled these few weeks fine, and I do plan to hand over more responsibility to him, but this next phase is delicate. I need to be at the helm. We have employees who count on us. There are contracts and—"

She gently placed a hand on his lips, silencing him. "Adam, I knew you couldn't, just as I think you knew what my answer would be. This brief summer thing's been magic, but it's over. I'd like to stay friends. Really, I don't want to lose that."

She tried to think of alternatives. She'd known he was leaving but really hadn't thought about what would happen in the aftermath. "Maybe you and Jessie could vacation here each year? I'd like a chance to see her grow up. My mother and father would love a chance to play grandparents regularly."

"Is there anything I can say to change your mind?"

She shook her head. "I'm afraid not. These last few weeks I've come to terms with some old resentments about my childhood, and I think I'm closer to my parents than I've ever been. But while I understand them better, it doesn't mean I can go along with it—I tried that with my marriage. It didn't work. As much as I care for you, I don't want to play second fiddle to Delmark. Dealing with the interruptions, the constant calls, the late nights. Eventually, I'd resent it too much. I don't want things to end on a bitter note for us. I'd rather say goodbye now and have a lot of fond memories of our time together."

"Then this is it." His voice was flat, devoid of any emotion.

Lee hated the distance that was now suddenly between them. "Yes. This is it. We both knew it was coming."

He didn't say anything, and when the silence grew too heavy, she whispered, "I'll miss you."

He blew out a long breath and stood. "Ditto. I don't want to draw this out. No long goodbye. I'm just going to finish packing tonight, then leave first thing in the morning."

"But I'll see you before you go?" She stood as well, just inches away from him physically, but so much farther away in reality.

Even when he leaned over and kissed her, she could feel the difference, the space that separated them. "Yes, you'll see us both."

"Then, I'd better let you get to it." She pulled away and started down the stairs.

"Lee?"

She stopped and turned.

"I wish you'd reconsider. We could come to Erie frequently. Vacation here. You'd come regularly and check on the store. We could make it work."

"Work is what it comes down to. You're devoted to your business, and now you've added a baby to the mix. I just don't see where we could fit in."

That wasn't exactly fair, and she knew it even as she said the words. She believed Adam would try to juggle it all, but she was afraid that in the end, his job would win.

She wanted him to say he'd stay. That he'd forget about the business, and stay with her, even though she knew he couldn't. Was it fair of her to ask?

"I'm sorry. I'll be over first thing in the morning to say goodbye," she said and rushed home.

Chapter Ten

Lee tried to blot out her final goodbye with Adam and Jessie. She hadn't cried…at least not until after his SUV pulled away.

She'd gone through the motions the rest of the day. She'd gone into work, sorted some beach glass, then closed up the shop and headed home.

Now, standing outside her cottage, looking at its empty twin, she couldn't go inside, so she sat on her porch and just stared at the lake. She felt as if there were a hole in her life. She'd lived with one for the last year, but she'd been right, it had finally healed. This hole, however, was new and open.

She missed Adam and Jessie.

Missed coming home to them.

Missed talking to Adam about her day.

Missed listening to Jessie.

She thought about a walk down the beach, but couldn't work up much enthusiasm.

"Hi, honey," her mother said as she rounded the corner of the house. "How was work?"

"Great. I sold a few pieces and have an idea for a new pin, so I guess it was productive."

Her mother slid into the chair next to her, the one Adam had sat in so often. "I brought you these."

Her mother handed her a stack of pictures. "I bought a printer for them. They're good aren't they?"

Lee thumbed through them. The one of her and her parents. Of Adam and Jessie. The three of them together. But the ones that really captured her attention was the series of her and Adam pulling Jessie from the water. The three of them. Laughing and wet.

"You miss him." There was no question in her mother's words, just utter certainty.

"Yes."

She expected her mother to start itemizing where she'd gone wrong and point out the steps she could take to fix the situation. Instead, her mother merely nodded.

"We do, too. He's a very nice man, and that Jessie…" She laughed. "That one is going to be quite a handful as she gets older. We hope he comes to visit now and again, because we'd like to see them both."

"We talked about them coming for holidays." But she realized he'd never promised. Maybe he'd rather just have a clean break.

The thought depressed her.

"Your father and I will be leaving soon as well. We think we're going to go to the Poconos for a few weeks, then maybe move into New England somewhere. We realized we've never seen New England in autumn. It's supposed to be breathtaking. After that, somewhere south for the winter."

"You'll be stopping in here again?" Lee was surprised how much she wanted them to.

"Yes. We just don't want to overstay our welcome. I know you're used to a certain measure of solitude. I also know you haven't had much at all in the last few weeks between Adam and Jessie, and us. But we'll be back…as long as it's okay with you."

"Of course it's all right with me."

Her mother reached over and took her hand. "We made mistakes, your father and I. But they never had anything to do with not loving you."

"I know that, too. I kept telling myself I was over all my childhood resentments, but I wasn't until recently. I am now. I'd love a chance to see more of you and Dad. I'd like to have a closer relationship."

"Us, too."

Lee realized her mother, her always strong and in

control mother, was crying. "So, about Adam. Do you have some advice?"

It was the first time she'd ever asked for her mother's opinion. Before, her mother had always been quick to offer, but this time she realized she really wanted to hear what her mother had to say.

"You'd think I would, wouldn't you? I know we've always told you how to build your business, how to live your life. It wasn't that we weren't proud of you, but rather we didn't know what to say to you. I've decided that simply saying, Lee, we're very proud of what you've accomplished, will suffice. You're a grown woman, a strong, intelligent woman who knows what she wants. I have no doubt whatever you do will be the right thing for you."

Lee hadn't realized how much she wanted to hear words like that.

"Thanks," was all she could manage to choke out.

"Of course, as much as I'd like to leave it at that, to not try and fix your life for you, I will say just one thing. Follow your heart. I wish I'd listened to mine more when you were growing up. That I would have worked harder at meeting your needs, not just the business's. Don't make that mistake with Adam. Don't let your rational reasons outweigh your heart."

"Mom," Lee began, but didn't know what she wanted to say.

Her mother seemed to understand. She patted her

hand. "Now, I have a route to plan. I'll leave you to your peace and quiet."

Her mother got up, then leaned over and kissed her cheek. "I know you'll work it out."

"Thanks, Mom."

Rather than just let her mother go, Lee reached out and threw her arms around her, hugging her tight. "I mean it, thanks."

"They were words that should have been said years ago. I'm just sorry it took us so long to realize it."

Lee sat in her rocker for the longest time, watching the sun set behind the lake. Emotions chased after logic, which chased after memories.

She wanted Adam and Jessie, but didn't want to be involved with another business-comes-first man.

She wanted them here, at the cottages, but that wasn't going to happen.

She looked through the pictures again. Her heart aching, wanting them both here with her.

This wasn't getting her anywhere, so she decided to stop trying. She sat back and concentrated on not thinking. But something had changed. It wasn't as peaceful as it normally was.

As a matter of fact, for the first time in her life, Lee felt…lonely.

She made herself a light dinner and looked forward to some relief from the pressing feeling while she slept, but even her dreams brought no comfort. She had the dream she'd dreamed so often over the years. Ever since she'd washed her face in the dew. But the dream had changed. Rather than dark and faceless, the man in her dreams was Adam. *Magic does exist,* he told her, as he had for years. But now he added, *Come to me, let me show you.*

Then she was working on a new necklace and a baby began crying. Unlike the earlier nightmares, Lee didn't ignore the sound. Instead, she jumped up and went to the crib where Jessie sat, holding out her arms to Lee.

She brought the baby to her and realized Adam was at her side.

Magic does exist, he repeated. *Let me show you.*

His dream request stayed with her as she woke. Only the request wasn't just a dream. Adam had really asked her to come, but she'd said no.

Why?

Erie was her home and she loved her cottage by the lake and her business, but…

There it was, that *but*. She hadn't exactly figured out *but* what, yet it was there. Big and looming.

Days passed as Lee tried unsuccessfully to get back to a normal routine. She walked the beach, worked on her jewelry. When that didn't help, she pulled out her sketch pad and tried to empty her mind with a drawing of the lake. She managed it, but without even thinking, she'd drawn a man and a toddler walking along the shore. Walking away.

She snapped the pad shut.

She'd said no. She knew it was the right decision. New York wasn't where she belonged. This was her home.

And as much as she knew it was true, it didn't feel quite as right as it always had.

She returned to the cottage and heard the phone ringing. She entered and snatched up the receiver.

"Hello?"

"Lee." Adam's voice. "I'm so glad we caught you."

She had a brief moment of panic. "Is something wrong?"

"No. I thought we'd call and say good night. Jessie has something to say to you."

She could hear the phone being jiggled, then Jessie's voice. "La, la, la."

"Isn't that great?"

"She learned to yodel?" Lee asked.

"No. That's your name. Lee. I was talking about you as I fed her dinner, and she just started. La la."

"My name?"

"I wished she'd said it before we left so you could have been there. But I thought a call was the next best thing."

Next best thing.

Lee knew she wasn't getting the best thing, just the next best.

"Thanks. It's wonderful." She could make out the la-las in the background growing fainter.

"Uh-oh. Gotta run. She's found a tissue box."

Lee was ready to hang up when she heard him utter a faint, "Miss you."

"Miss you, too."

He'd called and given her the next best thing. For the last year she'd pined for what she'd lost and tried to make do with the next best thing. And here she was, settling for it again.

Wasn't it time she insisted on the best thing?

Lee spent the evening making plans, plans that started with a call to Juliet and ended when she walked out to her parents' RV the next morning.

"Lee," her mother called, a smile on her face. "You got up early to come see us off?"

"No. Actually, I came to see how you felt about picking up a hitchhiker and taking a small detour on your way to the Poconos."

"Does this mean what I think it means?" her mother asked anxiously.

Lee nodded. "It does if you thought Juliet would take over the shop. Part of her wages will go toward buying a share in a full partnership. She'll deal with anyone who's interested in renting the extra cottage as well."

"And you?" her mother pressed.

"I'm heading to New York City. I could drive, but I know parking's crazy expensive there. And I could fly, but…" She didn't have time to finish the sentence.

Her mother bellowed, "Aston, hurry up and let's get this baby on the road. We've got a detour to make."

Lee watched as her cottage got smaller and eventually faded from sight. She'd miss it. Miss her quiet life on the lake. She'd grown up here. She'd come here, after she'd lost the baby, to heal. It had been home. But since Adam had arrived, things had changed. When he'd left, she'd realized that this wasn't home anymore. Home was wherever Jessie and Adam were.

The miles didn't seem to pass fast enough. And it wasn't just that she was anxious to get to Adam.

When Lee had come up with the idea of hitching a ride with her parents, it had sounded good. Logical even.

She'd worked so hard to take everything into account as she prepared for New York. But she hadn't prepared for the fact that her father was new at the whole recreational-vehicle-driving thing.

New and not so good at it.

By the time they reached the halfway point on Interstate 80, she discovered it was best to sit in the back of the RV and pretend she wasn't in a moving minibus with her father at the wheel.

When they finally started to hit New York traffic, even that didn't work. She tried to cope with her father maneuvering the RV through New York's congested streets by closing her eyes and visualizing the lake. Calm. Serene. The sound of waves.

Unfortunately, the sound of beeping horns far outweighed her ability to pretend.

She tried to pretend her nervousness was about seeing Adam, and though part of it was, truly, the main emotion she felt about seeing him was overwhelming excitement.

"Dad, really, I appreciate the ride, but I can take a cab the rest of the way."

"Nonsense," he scoffed. "The RV handles like a dream. Look how well she took that last corner."

By *well,* he meant he avoided hitting the taxi by a mere inch or two.

"Mom," Lee tried, looking for an ally.

"Lighten up, sweetheart. Life is an adventure."

Lee couldn't help smiling. She had never seen this side of her parents. As she thought about it, she wasn't sure if it had been there all along and old resentments had made her miss it, or if this was a new happy-go-lucky stage for her mother—but either way, Lee liked it.

"I'll lighten up if we make it to Adam's without an accident." Somehow, confessing she wanted a chance with him while wearing a body cast wasn't exactly what she had in mind.

"Have a little faith," her dad said. "Because, here we are."

"The receptionist said it was the sixth floor," her mother said.

"I just want to thank you both. For the ride. For coming to my house. For everything."

"Honey—" Her mother stopped, emotions playing across her face. "You don't have to thank family.... We love you."

She hugged them both. "Me, too. Wish me luck?"

"We don't need to. This is where you're meant to be. With Adam and Jessie."

"We're still heading to the Poconos, so we'll only be a few hours away. You call if you need us."

"Thank you. I'm so glad you started your retirement off in my backyard. I've always loved you both, but now I…" The word that came to mind was *like*. She liked them.

"You're stalling," said her mother. "Go get Adam. Send him our love."

Cars honked from behind the RV. "Yes. I'm going."

She picked up her suitcase, her purse and got out of the RV. She stood on the sidewalk and watched as her father eased the behemoth back into traffic and down the street.

She was going to miss them.

It was a new feeling, and she stood a moment simply appreciating it. Then she turned to study the skyscraper in front of her. She walked through the rotating door and spotted the elevator.

It was crowded with people. "Could someone hit six for me?" she asked as she wormed her way in.

Three stops later, the door opened and she got out

along with one other passenger. "Do you know where you're going, miss?" he asked.

"Delmark, Inc."

"The door's down this way to the right." He started walking with her.

"Thanks, but I'm sure I can find it."

"I'm heading that way anyway." He blatantly studied her as they walked, then broke out in a broad grin. "You're Lee, aren't you?"

"Darius?" she asked.

"Got it in one. You here for a visit?"

"I won't know for sure until I've talked to Adam. Is he in? I know I should have called first, but I…" She simply shrugged. She wasn't sure why she hadn't called. Maybe she feared he'd say don't come, although she knew that wasn't rational. Her coming to New York had been his idea, after all.

"He's at a meeting until after lunch, but why don't we put your stuff down in my office and I'll give you a tour, then take you to lunch while we wait."

"Really, I don't want to take up your time. I can just go do a bit of sightseeing, then come back."

"Are you kidding? I can't let you leave until he gets back. He'd kill me. And just think, if we start our friendship with you saving me from certain death, then I'll owe you. Not such a bad thing, that."

She laughed. "You do have a point. If you're sure I won't throw your entire day out of whack. I know how busy things are with branching out."

"Don't you worry." He led her through the outer office and stopped in front of the receptionist. "Lee, this is Amanda. Amanda this is—"

"*The* Lee?" the woman asked.

Darius nodded. "Whenever she comes, she gets right in."

"Like I'd keep you out." The gray-haired lady didn't look like Pearly Gates, other than the hair color, but she had a Pearly-esque feel about her. Like someone who could be counted on. "Doll, the entire staff is going to be so glad to hear you're here."

Lee shot Darius a questioning glance.

"Let's just say, Adam hasn't been his normal self since he came back."

Hazel made a snorting noise. "He's been a total ba…bear."

"Now, let's get on with your tour of Delmark, Inc. Then I'll take you out to lunch. Before Adam even gets back, you'll wonder how you could live anywhere but New York."

They stored her bag in Darius's office. He was a charming companion. He introduced her to the entire staff, showed her the Manhattan facility and blue-prints of the plant they intended to build.

"Have you bought property for it yet?" she asked. "I might not be an architect, but I can see it's going to be a huge facility."

"We made it bigger than necessary because we want room for future expansion. As for a location, that's Adam's department. But he's been working on something since he got back. Now, what about lunch?"

He took her to Grand Central Station. There was a beautiful restaurant on the upper level. Lee couldn't take in the entire scope of the building, so she concentrated on its pieces. The towering windows. Flags. The clock. But mainly, the people, all rushing, hurrying. It left her feeling breathless.

Darius kept her laughing throughout the meal. Telling her stories of Adam and the business.

"Did Adam tell you how we met?" Before she could answer, he continued, "He spoke at our school and, being extremely insightful and discerning, I latched on to him."

"I have a feeling it was a bit more mutual than that."

"No. He never had a chance. I was a pest. I can see it now, but he never let on. He gave me a job and he was the one who pushed me to go to college. He gave me what he termed a scholarship, but in actuality was a gift. He let me work around my classes, and when I graduated two years ago, he brought me in and…here I am. Vice president."

"He must have a lot of trust in your abilities."

"He's special. And I hope that's why you'll forgive me if I'm blunt. Don't see him unless you're going to stay. Leaving you…it's tearing him up. Don't put him through that a second time."

She paused, staring at Darius. "I'm here to stay."

"Great. Then let's head over and see if the boss is in."

"I meant to ask, what kind of meeting? That same important client that brought him back?"

"No. It's even more important than that. He tries to get home and have lunch with Jessie whenever he can. So he schedules his meetings in the morning, then lunches with her and comes back to the office."

Any worries about this being the right course evaporated as they walked together. Adam had every right to be proud of the business he'd built. She was sure that there would be long days and travel. But he tried to lunch with Jessie.

She smiled. "Let's hurry."

Adam had buried himself in paperwork. He worked hard to get out of the office by five o'clock every day, so he could have dinner with Jessie as well. It was tough, but it was worth the effort.

Jessie was thriving with the new situation. She basked in her grandparents' attention all day, and when Adam appeared, he showered her with his attention, saving any reports and memos until after she was in bed.

He knew there would be times he'd miss a dinner or lunch, but Jessie would always know he tried, that she came first.

Lee would be pleased.

He thought about calling, even went so far as to pick up the phone, then set it back down. If he told her, she'd think he was trying to butter her up to move here. She'd been adamant about staying in Erie.

Well, he had plans for that.

He opened the latest proposal for the factory. There was a light rap on his door.

"Come in," he called, not looking up. "Thanks Sheri. You can just put the figures on the table. I'll get to them next."

Someone cleared her throat. "Uh, I'm not Sheri, and I don't have any figures. But I do have a suitcase sitting in Darius's office, and a proposal."

"Lee?" He jumped up from his desk and hurried around, pulling her into his arms. "You're here. You're in New York. How long can you stay?"

He didn't wait for an answer, but kissed her instead. Knowing he'd never be able to find the right words to describe how he felt, he tried to convey the emotions in that kiss. He needed her to understand how much he'd missed her.

"Well," she whispered when they finally drew apart, "I'm happy to see you, too. And as for your question, how long I'm here depends on you."

"I'll have Darius get on the apartment right away, if it's still available. If not, you can stay with Jessie's grandparents maybe, until we find something else.

I—" He stopped. "I can't believe you're here. I never thought you'd leave home."

"But I'm not leaving home."

"Oh. Sorry. I must have sounded like a fool. But I'm confused."

"Adam, after you left, I discovered that my home is wherever you and Jessie are. So at this moment in time, it appears that New York is my home. And as for giving us a try, that's not what I want. What I want is for us to be a family. The three of us."

"Lee, that's what I was going to ask you. I just wanted to give you more time."

"I've had more time than you realize. Do you recognize this?" She reached beneath her shirt and pulled out a necklace. "It's the glass you left me that last day. My grandmother had told me if I washed my face in the dew the morning of my tenth birthday, I'd meet the man I'd one day marry. The man of my dreams. Then my archnemesis came along, and I…I pretended I had drops in my eyes and had to keep them closed."

"You didn't want to risk having to marry me?"

"Are you kidding? Back then I'd have rather kissed a toad than you. But, you left this for me and kissed me so sweetly on the cheek. And, I confess, I peeked as you walked away. So, you see, you have to marry me. It's been destined since I was ten."

"I'm the man of your dreams, eh?"

"Don't let it go to your head, Benton."

Adam laughed. He'd felt as if he were going through the motions until now, until Lee had come home to him. "I'm sure you won't let me. What about your store?"

"Juliet is taking over and will buy into a partnership with me. She's already talking about expanding the stock."

"You don't mind?"

She shook her head. "The store was always a means to an end. I worked to live, not lived to work, remember. I could take it or leave it. But my art, that's part of me, part of who I am. I realized that Delmark is part of you. It was selfish of me to ask that you give it up. Your passion for the business is part of what makes you you. And since I'm in love with you—"

"I swear, you and Jessie are more important than the company."

"But it's important, too. And that's okay. What's not okay is that you never did answer my question. Adam Mathias Benton, will you marry me?"

There was only one answer he could give her, this woman of his dreams. "Yes."

"Yes." She laughed weakly. "I didn't realize how nervous I was about your answer until you gave it to me."

"Yes was the only answer I could give. I was coming back to you."

"You were?"

He could hear the surprise in her voice. Didn't she realize how much she meant to him?

"The new factory? I've spent the day on the phone with the mayor of Erie, negotiating with the city for tax breaks. There's an old factory on Twelfth Street. I won't be there all the time, but I'll need to be there often, so you're not totally giving up your home. We'll be in Erie part of the year. You'll get to be home."

"I meant what I said, you and Jessie are my home. The only home I'll ever need."

He fingered the necklace, the small bit of glass. "You're sure?"

She kissed him then. "Positive. Adam Mathias Benton, you're the man of my dreams."

Epilogue

"There's something magic in the dew, Jessie," Lee said as she sat on the rock overlooking the lake, holding the sleepy toddler on her lap. "When you're older, I'll tell you the story."

A story about destiny…about love. She knew, without turning around, that Adam was behind her.

"Happy thoughts?" he asked, brushing her well-rounded stomach with his hand.

She turned and looked at her husband, the man she'd dreamed about for so many years. "The happiest."

"Ready to go home?"

"I'm already there," she assured him. She

looked at Adam and Jessie, as she placed her hand with the wedding ring on their unborn baby.

"I'm already there," she repeated.

* * * * *

HARLEQUIN®

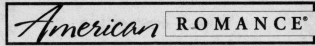

American **ROMANCE**®

IS PROUD TO PRESENT A
GUEST APPEARANCE BY

QUILL
BOOK
AWARD
WINNING
AUTHOR

NEW YORK TIMES bestselling author

DEBBIE MACOMBER

The Wyoming Kid

The story of an ex–rodeo cowboy,
a schoolteacher and their journey to the altar.

"Best-selling Macomber, with more than
100 romances and women's fiction titles
to her credit, sure has a way of pleasing readers."
—*Booklist* on *Between Friends*

The Wyoming Kid is available from
Harlequin American Romance in July 2006.

www.eHarlequin.com   HARDMJUL

If you enjoyed what you just read,
then we've got an offer you can't resist!

Take 2 bestselling love stories FREE!

Plus get a FREE surprise gift!

Page-turning drama…

Exotic, glamorous locations…

Intense emotion and passionate seduction…

Sheikhs, princes and billionaire tycoons…

This summer, may we suggest:

THE SHEIKH'S DISOBEDIENT BRIDE
by Jane Porter

On sale June.

AT THE GREEK TYCOON'S BIDDING
by Cathy Williams

On sale July.

THE ITALIAN MILLIONAIRE'S VIRGIN WIFE

On sale August.

With new titles to choose from every month,
discover a world of romance in our books written
by internationally bestselling authors.

HARLEQUIN *Presents*

It's the ultimate in quality romance!

Available wherever Harlequin books are sold.

www.eHarlequin.com   HPGEN06